SO-AAG-254

WHERE AGENTS FEAR TO TREAD

Following the critical success of the series featuring his
bookseller detective, Matthew Coll, Roy Harley Lewis
introduces a new hero, librarian Henry Franklin. But in
contrast to Coll, Henry is a dreamer, and anything but
tough. When his specialist expertise is needed to identify
priceless old Arabic manuscripts stolen from libraries and
museums and smuggled into Pakistan, Henry finds
himself embroiled in the terrifying world of fanatical
Arab nationalism, and international intrigue. The
unlikeliest of heroes, Henry survives murder and mayhem
through innocence and luck where seasoned agents fall by
the wayside.

WHERE AGENTS FEAR TO TREAD

ROY HARLEY LEWIS

St. Martin's Press
New York

Copyright © Roy Harley Lewis 1984
First published 1984

ISBN 0-312-86689-5

Library of Congress Catalog Card Number
84-50132

All rights reserved. No part of this book may be used or reproduced in
any manner whatsoever without written permission except in the case of
brief quotations embodied in critical articles or reviews. For information,
address St. Martin's Press, 175 Fifth Avenue, New York, N.Y. 10010

To Greg and Ruti

One

The explosion that tore down the massive gates of the desert fortress, signalled the turning point of the battle. As the Bedouin tribesmen burst in a never-ending stream through the smoke-congested opening, the handful of survivors of the only Legion outpost before Sidi Abbas withdrew to their last makeshift barricade. Grimly aware that the rebels of Ibn Shammah took no prisoners, they prepared for the inevitable outcome with courage and determination.

Only one man refused to acknowledge defeat. Contemptuous of the overwhelming odds, Sgt Ives Lamartine, stood his ground, defying the horsemen to do their worst. Firing with deadly accuracy, he unseated rider after rider until his ammunition was exhausted. Then, as the triumphant tribesmen converged, he grasped the hot barrel of his rifle with both hands and swung it as a club. The heavy butt smashed across the savage face of the first man, sending him crashing into the sand at his feet. A second fell and then a third, but the raiders came on. He felt a blow on his shoulder ...

Despite his preoccupation he could not resist the glimmer of a smile at the lightness of the blow, a mere tap. It seemed he was impervious to pain because the second felt little more than a push.

"Henry!"

Concentration gone, his mind stuttered, confused. The name was familiar, but surely his name was Ives ... Ives Lamartine?

"Henry! Didn't you hear me calling?" The voice belonged to a beautiful young woman who had no part in the fantasy, but he recognized her instantly. She was ...

Henry Franklin came to earth with a bump, turning in his swivel chair in an attempt to conceal the book he had been reading. But his secretary, Heather McNulty, anticipated the intention and snatched it from his grasp. "*Legion of Death!*", she exclaimed, almost triumphantly, as though he had been caught in possession of dangerous drugs. "And from the children's section! I can't imagine what people would say if they knew how the County Librarian spends his time?"

Henry wriggled under her stare. "We need to know what the kids are reading; what they want. How else can we have a satisfactory buying policy?" he protested, indignant at having to justify himself. But for someone who was invariably behind in his paperwork he knew that research 'inspired' by such Walter Mitty fantasies was difficult to explain, let alone justify. Besides, Heather not only worked for the library – she was also his fiancée.

He stole a surreptitious glance at her. At 28, four years his junior, Heather would not have been out of place in a Paris fashion salon. He was not the only person who wondered what . such a vision of loveliness saw in a gangling, pleasant-featured but prematurely balding and generally rather unprepossessing librarian. She was intelligent as well as beautiful, and as both sets of parents had pointed out, would make any man a perfect wife. He knew they were right. Heather had all the virtues, but occasionally he wished she was not always quite so serious. She was ambitious for her future husband; incidents like this prompted her to remind him that he was not dedicated enough. It was the term 'dedicated', when she really meant 'single-minded', to which he objected. He knew he was good at his job, and that his career was progressing satisfactorily. He still needed library experience but in due course he intended to specialize in his first love – manuscripts and early printed books in Arabic. He was already one of the country's foremost authorities.

But Henry Franklin was a romantic. He did not believe that a scholar was precluded from reading thrillers, or being a fan of Hitchcock. To him, old manuscripts were objects of beauty – but that did not stop him from admiring other forms of beauty. When they were together, Heather believed they should be doing something useful; she was setting him an example, by studying Arabic so that one day she might be of some assistance to him in his work. At such times Henry would need to force himself to concentrate, because he found her profile so captivating that he might just sit and stare, seeing her as Helen of Troy, Joan of Arc ... or, Pygmalion ... but then it was not difficult to see her as a marble statue.

It was Heather's seriousness, her solemnity, that took the edge off what he supposed was love. He had more fun with the most junior member of the staff, Betty Mailer, who had joined them last month as part of the Government's Youth Opportunities Scheme. Betty did not have the impressive academic background of most of the others in his team, but she might one day be a better librarian if – with his encouragement – she continued to study in her spare time. Betty seemed to like books and people in equal measure, and enjoyed introducing one to the other. Heather attributed his open but innocent affection for the girl as symptomatic of a retarded development.

He pulled himself together. Enough day-dreaming for one day. Heather was right. He could dream all he liked at night – in bed, when he was not wasting time. For the rest of the afternoon he would put the finishing touches to his detailed condemnation of the latest cuts in his budget, proposed by the philistine Finance Committee. Tonight he would have to do some further research into the minor variations in style and technique in early Arabic script. Some of the manuscripts sent to him had been damaged and were incomplete, and on occasion the text was almost indecipherable without the necessary continuity. Only the week before, in the absence of specific evidence he made assumptions in dating a thirteen-century scroll that later information proved to be almost two centuries out.

"There's a gentleman to see you – from the British Library," Heather announced, an undercurrent of excitement in her voice. It was Heather's considered judgement that Henry was wasting his talents in a public library, albeit at the County Headquarters, and although she grumbled at his lack of drive she never lost hope that as his reputation spread, the mountain would come to Mohammed. Being a serious young lady, she did not appreciate the significance of the comparison.

"British Library... ?" Henry echoed vacuously, wondering why anyone from that illustrious institution should have travelled thirty miles when they could have picked up a telephone.

In black jacket, sober pinstripe trousers and rolled umbrella, his visitor looked more like a senior civil servant than a custodian of books. In his late fifties, the man whose business card identified him simply as William Beckton, but gave no hint of his department or status, was an impressive figure. Only an inch or so shorter than Henry but carrying considerably more flesh on his large frame, his features were strong and sharply defined and there was a richness about the neatly trimmed whiter-than-white hair and moustache that gave him a clean, wholesome appearance ... the elder statesman one trusts instinctively. Most of the senior academics that Henry knew were far less personable ... nice, but rather blurred around the edges ... dog-eared, perhaps, like the books they cherished.

As usual his intuition was correct. As soon as Heather had left the room, Beckton confessed that he was not from the British Library. "It's only a white lie," he conceded, "although I don't actually work there, my department *is* responsible for certain matters relating to the library and the museum. Same with the V & A ... the Institute of African Studies ... and others."

"You're with the Government?" Henry speculated.

Beckton nodded affably, producing a plain buff file from his attaché case.

" ... That would be the Department of the Environment?"

His visitor, preoccupied with the papers he was trying to put in sequence, did not seem to hear him. At last he produced an elusive sheet and placed it on top of the pile. "Ah... ?" he declared, apparently satisfied. Henry was confused and about to ask the purpose of Beckton's visit when the older man anticipated the question. "I'm told you are one of the country's top authorities on Arabian manuscripts ... ?"

"Arabic?" interjected Henry helpfully, wondering if he was splitting hairs.

Beckton nodded. "Along with Douglas Johnston, Arthur Miles and Clinton Davis ... the difference being that they are actually custodians of a number of valuable manuscripts ... "

"Priceless," corrected Henry.

" ... some of the best collections we have in the United Kingdom ... or had."

"Had?"

"You must know about the spate of thefts?"

"Spate? I've heard of *two*, although that's bad enough."

Henry subconsciously grimaced at the thought of such fragile works of art being mishandled by thieves who had no real appreciation of the meaning of true antiquity. The one he had actually seen came from Egypt, and dated from 1411. Measuring some 61 x 25 cms it had been written and decorated in a kaleidoscope pattern of blues, reds, greens and gold by Muhammet, grandson of the great Yusef Hachiy. He had only seen a catalogue photograph of the other, a seventeenth-century manuscript of Ahhidi's "Diwan" with three miniatures in the Herat style attributed to Shah Qasim. He explained that the theft was common knowledge after his friend Doug Johnston had alerted the trade.

Beckton had worse news in store. "I'm afraid those were only the tip of the iceberg. There are over a dozen equally fine manuscripts missing ... "

"Do the police have any leads?"

Beckton's smile was sad. "They're doing their best, of course. But with all due respect, there is little they can do unless someone identifies the stolen material."

"Is that why you're here?"

The older man handed him the buff folder. "I'd like you to glance through these lists of missing books and their libraries. You'll know most of them."

Henry took the folder politely but did not open it. "There is no need, Mr Beckton. Anyone who came here trying to sell anything in this line would get his comeuppance. I would *know* if it was stolen; there's no need to check."

"We *know* where they are – at least, we think we do," Beckton answered.

Henry felt enormously relieved. "That's wonderful! Then why are you here?"

"I need someone with your qualifications to check our assumptions."

Henry raised an eyebrow. " ... I'm at your service, but isn't it simpler to ask the curators to whom they belong?"

Beckton's sigh was tinged with exasperation. "At this stage we cannot rule out the possibility there might have been some 'inside' help." He raised a hand to forestall Henry's protest. "I know your friends are all men of the highest integrity ... but stranger things have happened."

Reluctantly, Beckton conceded the point.

"The other reason is that they are not in this country any more."

Henry's puzzled expression betrayed his failure to understand what that had to do with it, and again Beckton seemed to read his thoughts. "It's not a question of just nipping over on the cross-channel ferry. They've turned up in Pakistan. Because of the amount of travelling involved – especially in the temperatures there at this time of year – we thought a younger man would stand up to the strain rather better. You've got ten years on the next chap. What d'you say?"

Henry's natural enthusiasm got the better of him. He relaxed and smiled broadly. "Assuming I could get the time off, I'd be delighted. Presumably I would be there for a few days and could do a little sight-seeing?"

"Naturally."

Henry's confidence grew. "If your department is meeting my expenses, perhaps I could buy an extra seat on the plane and take my fiancée? We may never get another opportunity to go as far as Pakistan on my salary."

Beckton smiled. He said nothing, but there was a note of authority in his eyes that made the question seem almost impertinent. Henry swallowed and changed the subject to enquire what sort of time scale Beckton had in mind.

"Tomorrow." It seemed from Beckton's instinctive response that the matter had already been decided. Before

Henry could protest that he needed a few days notice,
Beckton added: "My office will clear it with your committee
chairman, or whoever you like, this afternoon, so we may as
well get cracking. Any questions?"

Was that supposed to be a joke, Henry wondered. The cells of
his brain were already clogged as the questions, real and
half-formed jostled for attention. *Where* in Pakistan? In
what circumstances? *Who* would he be meeting? The
pictures swam past in disorder ... illiterate but dangerously
tough Pathan tribesmen, in some remote outpost in the
Khyber Pass – then men, not dissimilar to himself, more at
home in a university or smart hotel. What form would the
negotiations take? Would he be given a cash limit, or a free
hand, or ... Trying hopelessly to clear his head, he was
reduced to asking about flights and hotel accommodation.

To his surprise Beckton smiled, mistaking his
bewilderment for coolness. "I can see you're just the man
we need. We're not absolutely clear yet about our policy, so
if we decide to play it by ear, it's essential you give nothing
away. You're there as the expert; to tell us whether or not
the material on offer is the genuine article. Beyond that, all
decisions will be taken by your companion ... "

Companion? Henry did not know whether to feel irritated
or pleased at the news. He needed to calm down and start
again. "Perhaps you could give me some idea of the
sequence of events leading up to our trip?" he enquired.

Beckton nodded. "The details of the robberies – at the
four sites you'll know – are in that folder. They took place
within a few weeks of each other. Nothing else was taken so
it is obvious the thieves knew what they were after. Then
silence for about a month or so before there was an
approach to our cultural attaché at the embassy in
Islamabad. *Was the British Government interested in their safe
return* – for a price, of course ... "

"How did the material get out there?"

Beckton shrugged. "That's a police matter. My concern is with negotiations to get them back. For what it's worth, it seems the people behind it – and whether they used students or professionals doesn't really matter – are one of the Arab revolutionary groups. They say they need funds for peaceful revolution, and that while better-known bodies such as the IRA and Bader Meinhof rob banks, they merely take what was rightfully their property in the first place."

"They have a point," Henry interjected. "Most of the antiquities we drool over in the West were originally plundered by European armies."

Beckton laughed. "That's something the politicians can sort out. *We're* not out to redress the balance – at least, not on this trip. All we want from you is a decision on whether the manuscripts are the genuine article."

"Why should there be any doubt?"

"It isn't exactly a transaction between gentlemen," retorted Beckton, as though dealing with a child. "We don't trust them any more than they would us, if we asked for the goods to be handed over 'on spec'. They offered photostats, but since we're dealing with some remarkably delicate illumination we didn't think black and white was good enough."

"No one can be one hundred per cent certain without laboratory tests, but I should be able to tell. What about valuations?"

Beckton shrugged. "What about them?"

"We'll need to know in advance if there is any bargaining to be done. The only guidelines we have are the prices they fetched at the auction – and in most cases that was several years ago. Some could now be worth double. In specialist areas like this a document or book is worth whatever someone is prepared to pay, and that could be a half-million pounds – or next to nothing. If they're not too sure of their ground, it could be like a game of stud poker."

"You can leave all that to John Hamilton, the chap I was telling you about. Good man. Knows what to do in these situations. Speaks the language, of course … "

Which one? Henry wondered. His curiosity had been pricked. He did not bother to mention that he had taken Arabic as his main subject at Durham, and as well as being an authority on the language and its origins, he was reasonably fluent in several modern dialects. Instead, he enquired very casually:"He's been there before … ?"

Beckton hesitated. "I couldn't be certain … somewhere in the Middle East. I'm afraid I'm lost once one gets to Calais."

"Nothing to be ashamed of. I don't suppose 'one' gets the chance to travel much with the Department of the Environment?"

Beckton was busy fiddling with his attaché case on the floor and did not seem to catch the question. "I'll get him to phone you at home this evening." He stood up and extended a hand. He was about to move towards the door when he stiffened with what appeared to be a sudden recollection. "Oh Mr Franklin … I nearly forgot! We would rather you didn't mention the trip to anyone. It should only be a matter of three or four days, so you can say you've had to go to London … the British Library if you like … "

Henry was intrigued and mildly excited by the element of mystery, but Beckton's request was hardly practical. "Miss McNulty – my secretary – is also my fiancée. If I was in London she would expect me to keep in touch – in the evenings at least," he pointed out.

Beckton gave the problem no more than thirty seconds of his time. "I'm afraid I have to insist. Hamilton will give you a telephone number for her; if she calls, one of my people will know how to cope."

Henry began to feel uneasy, his excitement soured by an uncomfortable feeling of disloyalty to Heather. The degree of secrecy was irrational. Who did they think Heather was going to tell? The idea was ridiculous, of course, and he went through her circle of friends, starting with her mother ... her mother? Mrs McNulty was not exactly the most discreet of people. He reconsidered. It was a bore, and certainly unfair to Heather, but Beckton was probably right. His memory echoed Beckton's words: *three or four days*. It did not sound very much, and he could already imagine himself at next year's conference of librarians modestly giving an account of three or four *weeks* on the Indian sub-continent. He would have to ensure that he crammed as much as possible into that fleeting visit.

Two

Asked to describe major cities in a word, we might suggest that New York is *dynamic*; London, *stately*, perhaps; Paris, *romantic*; Rome, *beautiful*. All one can say about Karachi is that it is *big*, at least in the context of a population of seven million people. It is also hot, oppressive, overcrowded, and certainly no tourist paradise. Like any city, it does have its devoted admirers, but little of the character, charm, or even historic interest of so many places on the Indian sub-continent. Affluent in comparison with most cities, living conditions below the poverty line could not be much worse outside a disaster area; even above the line there are the extremes of rich and poor ... predominantly poor.

Although he should have known better, Henry Franklin was a romantic, and the more attractive images he clung to were those based on Kipling, and the just as dramatic true stories of the North-West Frontier, and of the Raj. He cared too much about the people to be happy at having his nose rubbed in the human misery and degradation, but Karachi was where their assignment took them so he was stuck with it. Aware of Henry's disquiet, Hamilton promised him a two-day trip to one of the old hill towns if they could quickly dispose of their commitments; and Hamilton was unquestionably a man of his word. Indeed, Henry was thrilled to be in the company of an intelligence operative; it was not something they could discuss, but he was reasonably certain that Hamilton belonged to DI6.

John Hamilton was everything that Henry in his daydreams imagined himself to be. He bore more than a passing resemblance to the movie actor who had re-created the Superman role; older perhaps, but enough to attract curious stares wherever he went; yet he was self-assured enough to seem unconscious of this attention. From his general behaviour, Henry guessed that he was extremely capable at whatever his undercover work entailed, but he treated the librarian with the respect due to an equal, albeit in a totally different world. Henry warmed to him instantly, and after a few hours in his company became relaxed and confident in what may not have been a dangerous mission, but one which was certainly not without a degree of excitement.

Hamilton filled him in on the background to the thefts, placing it in the context of a report prepared by his department on one of the Arab nationalist groups believed to be behind them. His briefing was knowledgeable, succinct and without apparent bias, although because of Henry's interest in all matters relating to the Arab world, he was more interested in the thirty-page dossier which he was able to read at his leisure on the long flight to Karachi. He was impressed by its scale and objectivity, pleasantly surprised that it could be the work of one of the Foreign Office's chinless wonders.

As a framework, it included all politically subversive groups throughout the Middle East, although the writer had placed less significance on the activities of those on the extreme left. The Mao, Leninist, Marxist and Anarchist factions were not only fragmented and constantly at each other's throats but had suffered from the inroads of groups from the Right, particularly from the rebirth of Islamic fundamentalism in Iran, whereas the more common ground shared by various "nationalist" groups held promise of a more sinister note.

The document stated: "There is undeniably a bond – racial, religious, ethnic, call it what you like, that makes an Arab-Muslim brotherhood potentially the greatest force in the history of mankind. The Cause is not new, of course, but in the last decade oil-riches have made what were once dream fantasies an achievable reality to the men who have devoted their lives to this end.

"The bond extends from Morocco, through Algeria, Tunisia, Libya, Sudan, Egypt, Jordan, Syria, Iraq, Iran, Lebanon, Saudi Arabia, to the principalities and sultanates around the fringe of the Arabian peninsula, as well as two major bastions in the North and East – Turkey and Pakistan. Europeans tend to associate Islam with the Arab states, or with the excesses of Khomeini's Iran, which is not Arab – but forgets that Pakistan is the most powerful Muslim state in the world, and Pakistan will soon have its own nuclear capability ... "

The author removed his report from the realms of speculation with a number of examples of the apparent inability of Arab nations to overcome personal rivalries – even in a popular common cause, such as a Holy War against Israel. But it listed the names of several men, currently in the background and little known, whose dreams transcended narrow national ambitions. If these were realized the course of history could be changed.

It was early morning when they landed, and Hamilton insisted that they get a couple of hours proper sleep in their rooms at the five-star Hotel Balimar, in Abdullah Haroon Road. Later when Henry had breakfasted, Hamilton telephoned his contact in Islamabad.

"Seems they're waiting for us," he announced, looking

none the worse for the long flight, while Henry felt as though he had not slept for a fortnight. "Obviously keen to get their hands on some hard currency."

Not feeling very talkative Henry took a large bite of toast and marmalade. Mouth full, he nodded politely.

Pouring himself a cup of coffee, Hamilton seemed to hesitate before continuing with the briefing. It was uncharacteristic. He stared at Henry, seeming to reappraise him, before remarking: "With any luck we shall have the whole deal sorted out by tea-time, but in this business one can never take too much for granted ... "

Assuming Hamilton was merely referring to the time factor – that there could be some bargaining which took longer than expected – Henry repeated his meaningless nod.

"Sometimes one can misjudge a situation; add what appears to be two-and-two, and make five. It's as well to be on our guard," added Hamilton.

"How do you mean?" Henry demanded, suddenly wishing he had not spread so much marmalade on his toast. He was conscious of a cloying sweetness that threatened to unsettle his stomach.

"I'm not really sure," conceded Hamilton. "I'd just like you to be alert."

Henry forced a laugh. "You don't have to worry about me. I would rather be in the picture. I may not have your experience, but I didn't just come for the ride."

Hamilton smiled reassuringly. "There's nothing to worry about. I'm inclined to be ultra-cautious by nature. I looked up the address in the street guide, and it's part of the old quarter of the city – not an area that tourists are encouraged to go – so keep an eye on your wallet ... "

"Oh ... " Henry was relieved, but tried not to show it.

They took a taxi across the city until the narrower streets became so congested with traffic they were reduced to a crawl and Hamilton decided it would be quicker to walk. He had the street map with him and most of the road signs were in English so they had no problem finding their bearings. By now the streets were little more than mud or sandstone tracks, so narrow that pedestrians were forced to hug the buildings on either side whenever a horse-drawn vehicle or the occasional car forced a way through.

On Hamilton's advice they walked in the centre of the road where possible, steering clear of the local inhabitants sitting on doorsteps and lounging in darkened passageways. As they approached their destination, Henry became increasingly aware of being watched; of the silent animosity of the local people; conscious too, of the camera in its expensive-looking case draped over one shoulder, temptation in itself. But there was no change in Hamilton's manner and he decided that his imagination was running riot. Even so he could not shake off the feeling of apprehension, and eventually discretion overcame his determination not to lose face. He communicated his anxiety to Hamilton, punctuating the remark with a short laugh to show that he still had the situation in perspective.

He had hoped that Hamilton would share the joke, but his companion did not even look at him, his eyes continuing to scan the road and buildings ahead. "Only fools don't know the meaning of fear, Henry. As I said before, no harm in being alert. To be on the safe side, keep near me ... not too near those houses ... "

Henry was only too aware that even in the centre of the road they were only a few yards from either side, but before he could comment, Hamilton continued: "I don't want you suddenly dragged off through a doorway. If we keep together in the middle, we'll be better able to handle an attack."

Attack? Henry's heart dropped to his boots where it was

joined by his stomach. He wondered if there was a public lavatory within striking distance – and then if he could face the sort of toilet one might find in this district. He looked desperately at his companion for moral support, but Hamilton seemed so unconcerned that he forced himself to keep the panic at bay, and his legs, as well as his bowels, under control.

Simple though Hamilton's instructions were, they were difficult to follow because the road now was scarcely wider than an alleyway. At last Hamilton pointed to the house they wanted. As they drew nearer, Henry's apprehension mounted – yet even so he was surprised when the attack came. While their eyes scanned the shadows the menace came from above.

Hamilton sensed the danger first, instinctively looking up just in time to see a huge Persian rug, weighted at the four corners, floating down from a rooftop. He yelled at Henry to dive for the side but plummeting quickly like a crash-landing magic carpet it was on them before they could get out. Because of the weights it retained its full width – stretching to both sides of the road – leaving, as Hamilton had anticipated, only two possible avenues of escape. Henry did not have time to see how his more alert companion had made out before going down under the carpet's cumbersome mass.

Henry assumed that Hamilton reacted like the trained agent he was, but he was a scholar. Forgetting that his life was in danger, his first thought was for the magnifying-glass in the inside breast pocket of his jacket. It had been a twenty-first birthday present from his parents when he was beginning to take an interest in old manuscripts, and had remained a faithful companion over the years. He snatched the glass from its resting place and held it at arm's length as his body hit the ground. It was only then he remembered the camera, although he was reasonably confident it would be protected by its leather case. However, his relief at knowing the magnifying-glass had escaped damage was short-lived.

The spontaneous action saved his life because his attacker – believing the object in the victim's hand to be a gun, slashed at it through the carpet with the knife that had been intended for Henry's body. Although the blade, slightly deflected by the carpet, slid off the silver rim of the magnifying-glass, the downward momentum forced it on to the ground where the glass disintegrated. Enraged, Henry bucked like a wild stallion at the body trying to restrain him, and succeeded in dislodging it. The sudden weight on top of the carpet towards the centre enabled him to scramble clear from the side, and he emerged like a rocket, blinking at the sudden brightness.

Even as he collected his wits, Henry saw that his attacker had also regained his feet and was advancing with knife outstretched. He was conscious of not being actually afraid, yet his limbs were frozen as though he was being held in suspended animation. Transfixed, he stared at the lightly tanned Pathan hoping for some indication of fallability, or that he might change his mind, but the intense expression on the bony unshaven face with only the moustache neatly trimmed, seemed to belong to an experienced assassin. Any remaining doubt was dispersed by the way he held his knife, low down with the blade uppermost.

Henry knew that he was no match for an armed assailant but his only possible hope of salvation was to run away, and his legs were paralysed. The man was within a couple of feet of him when he stopped in his tracks, stiffened and grunted with shock and pain before collapsing at Henry's feet – a knife protruding from between his shoulder blades.

Looking up with a mixture of horror and relief, Henry

realized that his saviour was Hamilton – the companion he had completely forgotten in his panic. With his back to the wall of one of the houses, Hamilton was fending off three attackers and looking no more bothered than if he was working out in the gymnasium. He was fighting for his life and Henry could not imagine how he had found time to watch for him too, but his manner was icy cool and unhurried; his concentration the product of years of training and experience. One native already lay prostrate at his feet and as Henry watched with admiration another who had ventured too near was felled by a karate chop to the Adam's apple.

Hamilton was still being pressed by the other two, and Henry suddenly found himself inspired to lend a hand. But as he moved forward, the agent spotted his intention and ordered him to stay out of the fight. "I'll handle this, Henry," he shouted. "It's my responsibility!"

Henry hesitated, aware that he might only impede his friend. However, he felt a moral obligation to do *something*, if only to offset the possibility that Hamilton might be defeated by sheer bad luck. Spotting the knife that had been used to kill his attacker, he did not stop to think and pulled it from the dead man's flesh, wiping the blood fastidiously on the grimy shirt. Then gripping the point of the blade between the tips of the fingers of his right hand, he threw the knife in the style of the professional circus acts he had seen on television. He aimed for the back of one of Hamilton's assailants marvelling at his natural skill as it flew unerringly towards its target. Until now he had never hurt – let alone killed – anyone, but moral judgement was suspended as he marvelled at his own hitherto untapped resourcefulness. Fortunately for his subsequent peace of mind, the aim was not as perfect as he had assumed, but it was near enough to clip the man's ear, more than enough to unnerve him. His resolve gone, the man was no match for Hamilton who disabled him with a kick in the groin, followed by a chop to the neck as he went down. The remaining member of the gang threw in the towel and hurried away, unmolested by Hamilton.

"Well done, Henry," Hamilton declared, and the librarian suddenly felt marvellous. The adrenalin being pumped into his bloodstream made him feel like giving chase to the surviving member of the gang, but Hamilton was too professional to allow anything to delay their own departure. "The police could be here within minutes; we don't want to get involved. If we can't get away in time, we must say that we were attacked by thieves, and that we were on our way to report the incident."

Knowing that as Europeans they could be identified more easily, they took a mini-tour of Karachi, changing taxis a half-a-dozen times before returning to their hotel. Hamilton did not speak more than a few words throughout the journey, brooding on the way he had allowed himself to walk into a trap. Still elated by their escape, Henry was put out initially by his friend's preoccupation, until he realized that there was no longer any reason for his presence. Did this mean he would be returning to London on the next available flight, or would Hamilton be able to pull something out of the fire?

Hamilton still seemed despondent when they returned to their hotel. Dispensing with his customary discretion, he signalled Henry to accompany him to his room while he telephoned the embassy in Islamabad. Yet when he had been connected with Colonel Crawford's extension, he did not speak until the Cultural Attaché had acknowledged the call for the third time. There was a note of exasperation in the voice by the time Hamilton responded.

" ... It's me," Hamilton eventually conceded. Pointedly

he held the receiver away from his ear so that Henry could eavesdrop.

There was only a momentary pause before Crawford replied: "How did it go?" He had an affected drawl, accentuated by some distortion on the line.

"It didn't," Hamilton said, his voice expressionless. "We were ambushed *en route* ... "

The voice at the other end took on a peevish note. "Ambushed? Are you serious?" He answered himself with a reproof. "Of course, you are ... I'm sorry! Are you all right? What about your little librarian, Mr er ... er ... ?"

Henry grimaced, but Hamilton laughed. "Don't concern yourself about our 'little' librarian – he's the last of our worries. I've never seen such a cool customer outside the department. Couldn't have managed without him."

Henry glanced at him sharply to see if the agent was pulling his leg, but the poker expression had returned. Giving him the benefit of the doubt he allowed himself to be uplifted by Hamilton's apparent respect, no matter how undeserved it was. In other circumstances he might have protested that his contribution was exaggerated, but he sensed that Hamilton was in no mood for splitting hairs, and that there was something significant in the telephone conversation.

He was vaguely aware of Crawford's reaction, apparently impressed, and then the attaché asking why, if they had been unhurt, they had not proceeded to their appointment?

"Because that was where we were attacked! It was a set-up, Crawford." His voice was still without expression, but Henry thought he detected an undertone of menace.

"Set-up?" Crawford echoed.

"Trap."

"That's impossible. It could only have been an unfortunate coincidence."

"I'm not speculating, Crawford. I'm *telling* you. They weren't just muggers – I had to kill one! Who knew about the meeting?"

"No-one, of course."

Hamilton's eyes switched to Henry, although his mind was already elsewhere, his brain on automatic control. The librarian returned the stare with admiration. He felt privileged to be on the same team. Not only was he as physically accomplished as any fictional spy, but he had the brains to hold his own in the more complex world of intrigue and double-dealings. Henry suspected he was hinting to him that they had been betrayed by the Cultural Attaché, but was playing for time until he had more evidence.

"Well, Crawford: if we assume it wasn't *you* who set us up," he was saying, "you had better check on the Embassy staff and find out of your telephone is being bugged ... "

"This is terrible," protested Crawford, "I shall have to tell Sir Arthur at once."

"You do that. But first get back to your contacts, and find out what's going on. If you're sure it wasn't them double-crossing you, make the next meeting somewhere safer."

"You will stay then?"

"Depends on what you come up with ... ?"

"Perhaps you had better lie low for a while?"

"We shall see," Hamilton replied.

"For your safety, quite apart from the risk of you being identified if there is a murder enquiry. The last thing the Embassy wants at the moment is a scandal ... "

A flicker of anger registered for a moment on Hamilton's face. "I said we'll see!" he repeated, his voice under tight control. "Ring me back here as soon as you've made contact. In fact, ring us back anyway – we'll wait." He sighed as he replaced the receiver.

"You don't trust him?" Henry enquired.

Hamilton shrugged. "The first rule in this business is: when in doubt trust *no-one. Somebody* didn't want us to keep that appointment."

An hour passed but there was no call from Crawford. Uncommunicative, Hamilton sat lost in his thoughts and before long the general air of gloom began to affect Henry Franklin. The room's air conditioner was creating such a din that he switched it off. The air was oppressive, but it was still relatively cool so he threw open the window shutters and stood out on the balcony. The view along the tree-lined avenue was impressive. He called to Hamilton. "It's quite a picture ... take a look to the East ... "

Hamilton joined him by the open window. He said nothing but his expression indicated that he shared Henry's appreciation of one of the City's more pleasant sights. When he staggered back a few moments later, Henry was not alarmed but it was the ominous "thwack" of a rifle a split-second later – too clipped to be a car backfiring, even to his uneducated ear – that confirmed his worst fears. He looked round at Hamilton, thrown back against the foot of the bed. There was a distinctive neat hole in his forehead ... a hole that became more blurred until it exploded into blackness as Henry fainted. The unconscious movement saved his life, because the bullet aimed for his head was at least six inches too high.

Three

The police officer who came to take Henry's statement was a swarthy, heavily pockmarked Detective Inspector in his middle forties. To the Englishman, shattered by the sudden demise of his friend he had believed to be larger than life, and feeling very much alone, Zia Khan's ugliness was strangely comforting. The policeman's ravaged face registered the impact of life's vicissitudes; it had seen too much and had been too abused to be anything but honest. He was also courteous, well spoken in an unpretentious way, and apparently unflappable.

Henry tried to be helpful, but had to concede that Khan did not appear very convinced by his account of the shooting. He seemed in turn attentive, sanguine, impatient, tired and after half-an-hour even a fraction desperate -- anything but satisfied. In common with almost any detective in almost any city he did not have the time to cope with the routine crime on his 'patch', let alone the out-of-the-ordinary to downright bizarre. The trajectory of the bullet in the dead man validated the Englishman's wild story of shots from a nearby building, but a search of the premises opposite had been fruitless; too late to find a gunman hanging around, nor turning up any other clue either.

He paced back and forth to the balcony, hinting on more

than one occasion that an assassin across the street could not have a clear view into the room – unless someone had opened the shutters at just the right time. Henry's account sounded more contrived every time he repeated it. Here, people learned to live with noisy air conditioning, and Khan implied that if his colleagues had not found a second bullet, he might have come to the conclusion that the shutters were opened as a signal. "The statement you have signed is a full and *complete* account of what happened, Mr Franklin?" he asked, as though resigned to the fact that the truth was too much to expect.

"Absolutely," Henry insisted.

"There is nothing that could have slipped your memory? After all, it must have been a traumatic experience ... "

"Yes ... I mean 'no', nothing."

"Let me be frank with you, Mr Franklin. People assume that police officers must be very clever to catch villains and murderers. It is not so – at least, not necessarily – because, in general, human behaviour changes very little over the centuries – *details*, perhaps, but not fundamental factors like motives and methods ... "

Henry listened politely, wondering what it had to do with him.

" ... Take the average tourist, for example. Statistics tell us that the average tourist is unlikely to be involved in bank robberies or crimes of passion ... in short, anything that might take weeks or months to plan, or to fester. Note that I am referring to the *average* tourist ... "

Nerves were already turning Henry's stomach inside-out, and he hoped he would not be forced to dash to the lavatory. Hopefully, the bilious look might pass for concentration due to his intense interest in what the inspector was saying.

"It is different with the other sort," Khan went on. "In

those cases we could get a phone call telling us to drop the enquiry like a hot potato, to leave it to ... well, those who deal with these things. Very frustrating at times, Mr Franklin."

Convinced that Khan suspected the truth, Henry felt himself nodding until it became a nervous reflex.

"Of course they can't just ignore us. If the crime is serious – such as murder – we have been known to dig our heels in. I expect it is much the same in your country, Mr Franklin ... rivalry between the police and the security people?"

Henry shrugged. "I suppose so. I don't know much about these things. I am a librarian. Nothing like this has ever happened to me before."

"According to your passport you do not travel very much – not like your friend, Mr Hamilton."

"I believe he was an export manager; that would account for it ... "

"Is *that* what he told you?"

"I think so. So much has happened in the past few hours, I can't really be sure what he actually said."

"But you were more than casual acquaintances ... you booked into adjoining rooms in the same hotel."

"We got talking on the plane. He mentioned the Balimar and I was only too pleased to take his advice."

"Oh? I thought they said the rooms were booked in advance. Perhaps I misunderstood. I must admit I was a little surprised that you did not prefer a 'package' tour? Most tourists seem to find them more convenient when they don't know a country."

Henry shrugged. "My requirements are probably different to most people. I'm not interested so much in the popular tourist haunts as places of antiquity ... your libraries and museums, for example. I'm a bibliophile, and something of an expert on old manuscripts."

Khan appeared to accept the explanation on its face value. "So once installed here, you and Mr Hamilton went your separate ways?"

"Yes ... " Henry hesitated. "Just before he was shot, I was just asking ... picking his brains ... before starting my schedule. He knew Karachi ... "

" ... Comparing notes?"

"In a sense."

"Can you be more explicit?"

The Englishman shrugged, at a loss for words. "How do you mean?"

"Well, for example, there was an incident reported earlier today: two Europeans were attacked in another part of the city. It seemed such a remarkable coincidence that I thought it might have been you ... and Mr Hamilton ... ?"

"As a matter of fact it *was* us," Henry replied, wriggling with embarrassment. "I suppose I should have mentioned it earlier."

"Earlier?"

"To you, that is. I wouldn't have bothered the police in the normal way. Someone tried to snatch my camera. I shouted for help and some of the local residents came to my rescue. It all became rather heated, and unfortunately a fight started – so we slipped away. If we had seen a policeman it would have been different, but since we hadn't lost anything we didn't make a point of it."

Khan stared at him in disbelief. "And you do not think it strange that less than twenty-four hours of arriving – before you had time to make any enemies – you have been attacked not once, but twice! Short of managing to offend someone in the plane, or at the airport, there is only one possible explanation – it was a case of mistaken identity!"

Henry approved of the theory. "That's it! We must have been mistaken for someone else?"

Khan's face relaxed into the semblance of a smile: "In the absence of an alternative explanation, I shall have to accept that premise – at least, until enquiries in the United Kingdom are completed. You were not thinking of leaving Karachi for the time being?"

"Well ... yes. As you say, it's been a shock. I'm not really sure I wouldn't like to get home as soon as possible."

Khan raised an eyebrow. "The cost of a return flight from London is not inconsiderable. It would be a pity to waste it ... ?" His eyes posed the unasked question, but Henry did not rise to the bait as he added: "That is your business, of course. I shall do my best to see that we do not keep your passport any longer than necessary. Until then it would be sensible to remain at the hotel. We will keep an eye on the place."

"But you can't withhold my passport," Henry protested. "I'm a British subject ... " Suspecting that he was being pompous, as well as totally ineffectual, he stopped in mid-sentence.

"Speak to your embassy," Khan advised, his manner conciliatory. "That is why they are there. Do you know anyone at Islamabad?"

Henry hesitated before deciding it was safer to plead ignorance.

Inspector Khan needed only a moment's reflection before suggesting that he telephone someone called Don Beveridge. "Helpful sort of chap," he said. "We send him a few stranded hippies from time to time."

When he had gone, Henry was torn between relief that the questioning had come to an end, and anxiety that he was now alone, hopelessly vulnerable should Hamilton's killers decide to finish him off too. He needed advice but was wary of giving a stranger like Beveridge – "helpful chap" that he might be – the full story without an appreciation of

Hamilton's true status, or how sensitive the assignment had been. Crawford had been the contact, but having observed the way Hamilton had behaved on the telephone, he was even more suspicious of him. It might be better to do nothing in the hope that Beckton would get him off the hook. He recalled Beckton's face ... the open, honest look ... and the palms of his hands began to perspire. If there was the slightest chance of Her Majesty's Government being compromised or embarrassed by any sort of scandal, he had no doubt that for all his apparent integrity Beckton would drop him like a hot potato.

He wondered how what seemed to have been a routine operation could have gone so disastrously wrong. It depended on what one meant by routine! Would an agent of Hamilton's calibre be needed to buy back a few old manuscripts? And since when, with libraries starved of finance, had the Foreign Office – D16, or whoever they were – been philanthropic enough to allocate funds to retrieve stolen property? He wondered if he had been conned all down the line, and longed to speak to someone he could really trust. Suddenly he was missing Heather, even though he suspected she might have been annoyed with him for having behaved with such innocence.

Eventually he could no longer stand the suspense of doing nothing; he took the inspector's advice and phoned the helpful Beveridge. The embassy official promised to "see what could be done" – and promptly passed the buck to Crawford, but at least his indecision had been resolved for him. The colonel's tone gave little away, but he sounded cool and efficient, and the element of authority was strangely reassuring, when he instructed: "Stay where you are; say nothing and do nothing until I arrive on the morning flight." He reminded Henry of a family solicitor, and it must have been the knowledge that someone was coming to take charge, that helped Henry get a few hours of restless sleep.

After breakfast, faced with the prospect of a morning spent commuting between his small room and the not much larger hotel reception area, Henry took a chance and ventured out for a stroll. Delighting in what was for him the rare experience of a hot sun cooled by a light breeze from the Arabian Sea, he draped jacket and camera over one shoulder and rubbernecked like the tourist he was supposed to be. But when the novelty began to wear off, the events of the past few hours began to return, and he felt a flicker of apprehension every time he caught a stranger's eyes. He returned to the hotel earlier than intended, and by the time Crawford arrived he was beginning to appreciate the meaning of claustrophobia.

Crawford looked what he was – a retired army officer. Although he knew he was jumping to conclusions, Henry suspected that the colonel was the D16 representative at the embassy, and his role as Cultural Attaché merely a façade. He doubted whether the man had read a book, apart from military manuals in his adult life, and he would have looked distinctly out of place in a theatre or cinema. He was a stiff-backed, spiky individual who made it clear from his opening remarks that he resented being saddled with problems which might never have arisen if 'London' had not been so high-handed.

"But I thought they were merely responding to your ... Well, wasn't it you who said the stolen manuscripts had turned up in Karachi?"

"That's why I'm here – to provide information. Most of it does not require any sort of follow-up. When it does the situation should be evaluated on its merits. This was perfectly straightforward and I thought they had enough sense to realize that the man on the spot was best equipped to handle it. Everything was under control, and if I needed assistance I would have asked ... "

Henry did not consider he was qualified to defend 'London'; only to justify his own presence. "I'm sure you are right, but it was nothing to do with me. I'm only an after-thought – the expert brought in to check the manuscripts were genuine ... "

"I'm not concerned with you," Crawford interjected, without a thought for Henry's feelings. "My objection was to Operation Overkill – sending their big guns when it merely needed a little negotiating – something I could have done standing on my head. With these subversive groups it's a question of the devil they know; in this part of the world I'm known *and* respected. Professional killers like Hamilton would have scared the wits out of them ... "

"He didn't get much of a chance," Henry pointed out, indignant that Hamilton could not defend himself.

"Precisely. When rats think they're cornered, they are scared enough to attack. Now we've probably lost contact with them ... "

No word of remorse over Hamilton's death; no hint of sympathy to the survivor. Henry's irritation got the better of his nervousness to ask how the killers could have known about their arrival in the city.

Crawford sniffed, his general manner patronizing. "Obviously you know very little about this business. Don't assume that because they are foreigners ... Wogs, at that ... they are not every bit as efficient as us. Since this is their home territory it's that much easier too; contacts all over the place. The tip-off probably came from someone at Immigration."

Henry's confusion was complete. Perhaps Hamilton, for all his experience *had* over-reacted? Presumably Beckton trusted his man on the spot? "As you say, I don't understand these things," he conceded. "What do *you* think I should do? The police have confiscated my passport for the time being."

Crawford shrugged. "Normal procedure. I understand from London that you're completely clean, so you should have it returned within a couple of days, with any luck. Meanwhile, it's too dangerous for you to stay here. They might have another go."

"Inspector Khan told me to stay put."

"He probably meant well," Crawford said, his manner making it clear he was not in the habit of taking the advice of foreigners, "but he is not in possession of the full facts. We'll take care of the police if it should arise. My main concern is to keep you out of harm's way."

Henry's anxiety returned. "You know much more about these things ... I'd be grateful."

"Good man. I'll give you the address of a safe hotel ... not very pretentious, I'm afraid, but you can put up with it for a couple of days ... until your passport is returned."

"Of course."

The colonel opened his brief case, produced a padded envelope, and from it took out an automatic pistol. "The place *is* safe, but I don't believe in taking any chances. *Nothing* is completely safe – even Buckingham Palace. You had better take this ... give it back to me before you leave for London."

Henry waved the gun away. "I wouldn't know what to do with it."

"Nonsense! A child could handle it. Bit heavy perhaps, but you know what I mean. Try it for size."

Gingerly, Henry took the gun. It *was* heavy. The shape, particularly the distinctive barrel, was familiar; perhaps he had seen a photograph, or read a description in one of the Bond thrillers. "It's a ... isn't it a Luger?" he asked.

Crawford glanced at him sharply, and then relaxed. "You almost had *me* convinced for a while. I should have realized that Beckton would not send an incompetent idiot – especially after what Hamilton said about you."

The misapprehension was impossible to refute. *I am* an incompetent idiot, Henry silently protested, realizing that Crawford would no longer accept the truth. "Colonel Crawford," he announced, drawing himself to his full height, hoping that it would add authority to his words. "I'm not terribly concerned about your opinion of me. I'm a librarian – not one of your colleagues. If it eases your conscience, I'll take the gun, but I can't answer for the consequences if I should have to use it."

Crawford nodded impatiently. "It's German, as you guessed. Can't be traced to us, so *if* you have to use it – just dump the thing. Whatever happens, don't be caught with it in your possession."

Henry glared at him; it was obvious he had not listened to a word. The colonel meant well, perhaps, but Henry disliked him. He could not wait for the days to pass until he was on the flight back to London.

The water from the hot tap, shuddering and whining with the effort, was lukewarm and discoloured. But it was water and since the cold tap did not work at all, Henry was grateful. Cupped in his sweating palms, it was surprisingly cool and soothing as he bathed his eyes. The lids irritated naggingly, and he wondered if there had been any sand on his pillow. It was everywhere else.

Crawford's warning that the place was 'unpretentious' had been a masterpiece of understatement. It was a filthy, flea-bitten hovel that had not seen an ordinary tourist for twenty years; it reminded him of a 1940s film with the only white man in residence – a villainous Peter Lorre, trafficking in drugs. He longed to go out, but Crawford had been adamant; consoling him with the knowledge that he had only another day or so to endure. His wristwatch seemed to come into its own; time dragged and watching the hands change was almost an interest in itself. Henry never went anywhere without a handful of paperbacks – but for the first time in his life, he found he was fighting a losing battle with the print.

It had become such an ordeal that when there was a gentle knock at the door of his room it was an incredible relief. For all its faults the place was safe. Crawford had assured him that the owner could be trusted; he must try not to be put off by the man's total disregard for personal hygiene. Another instinctive glance at his watch was reassuring; barely four o'clock and Karachi as yet had not stirred from her summer afternoon lethargy. The world outside the tiny, cell-like room was tranquil, and if deceptive, then at least a charming and inevitably disarming deception. At the second knock, undemanding, even obsequious, he rose from his ugly iron bedstead and walked over to the door, wrinkling his nose at the prospect of that pungent odour on the other side of the door. Yet even as he opened it a couple of inches, he realized he had blundered; a simple, thoughtless error of judgement.

There was nothing in the appearance of the two strangers that need have alarmed him; they did not wear masks, or carry guns – but he was apprehensive, and his brain struggled to keep pace with the intuition on which he depended now that he seemed to be living in such a different world. He had anticipated the arrival of Hamilton's killers countless times in his imagination, but not men like this.

In those laboured seconds he studied the strangers. There seemed little doubt they were Pakistanis, but presenting a stark contrast in appearance. The man who stood slightly in front was very light-skinned, his aquiline features strikingly handsome, and almost certainly a Pathan from the North-West Frontier territories. The ethnic origins of his companion was more difficult to determine; a giant, scarcely less than six feet six inches tall and weighing in the region of 250 lbs, he was like a villain from a strip cartoon – his head completely shaven or bald, and his face criss-crossed with scars and pockmarked. The features reminded Henry of Inspector Khan, but in comparison with the policeman's rugged ugliness, there was a nightmarish look about this man. His eyes were dark brown, practically black, so that from a distance the pupils seemed dilated; an illusion but disconcerting. He was wearing a well-cut pin-stripe grey flannel suit of good quality, but at least one size too small for him, and his long arms protruding from the sleeves seemed disproportionately long, giving him an ape-like appearance.

The smaller man, obviously the leader, immaculately dressed in a brown tweed English suit, spoke first, with a question: "Mr Franklin?"

Henry nodded cautiously, automatically putting his right foot behind the door. But when the visitor continued, politely: "Can you spare a few moments?" he was lost for words. The killers could have blasted him in the doorway – through it, if necessary. Conscious of his indecision, he hedged. "What do you want? I'm rather busy."

The softly-spoken stranger's smile was disarming. "I should like to talk to you, Mr Franklin ... " His shrug had the eloquence of a diplomat. "It is a little ... uncomfortable on the landing." The manner was soothing; yet without waiting for an answer he seemed to glide into the room. Half-heartedly Henry told himself that they had merely expressed a desire to talk with him, but the intuitive doubts were more positive, and almost immediately Henry had reason to regret his indecision.

While he kept his eyes on the visitors' spokesman, the giant moved unnoticed behind him, as though by instinct straight to a bedside cabinet drawer from which he removed the Luger. His companion spoke to him hastily in Urdu and then turned again to Henry, smiling apologetically. "You must forgive my friend – he is a little nervous of guns. It will be returned to you before we leave." He looked pointedly at a chair. "May we be seated?"

The request seemed oddly out of place in the spartan bareness of the room; apart from the bed, one rickety wooden fold-up chair. It was not expected that the sort of person who stayed here would ever be entertaining.

The giant – Henry assumed he was a servant or bodyguard – took up a watchful station with his back to the door, leaving the solitary chair as a shabby status symbol. Henry had no alternative but to stand, or, as had quickly become his custom, sit on the bed. He did so now and immediately regretted it. At least when he was standing, his height counted for something – in fact the size of the man by the door put his own height in perspective; for the first time in years he did not feel freakish. But his balance on the bed was somewhat precarious, and if there was one thing he needed now it was a little dignity.

Drawing his knees up in front of him in a show of relaxation, and as positively as he could – but having to concentrate to prevent the words from tumbling out nervously – he asked who they were.

Posing the question, he studied the man who faced him. On closer inspection, the good looks were somewhat stereotyped, a little *too* striking. Jet black hair brushed back – no oil, admittedly – from a high forehead ... straight nose and pencil-thin moustache. His complexion was sallow more than tanned, but the eyes were distinctive, a surprisingly light blue. In another time and place, the man might have passed for a gigolo, but Henry sensed that he was intelligent and tough. He noted too, that when he smiled, the blue eyes remained impersonal.

"I can understand your surprise, Mr Franklin – but I will explain ... Unlike you Anglo-Saxons, we have learned to come to terms with Time. Perhaps it has something to do with the climate."

The feeling that the man was prolonging the tension, even gaining some pleasure from it, helped keep Henry's panic at bay. He could not imagine a professional like Hamilton being anything but totally dispassionate at all times. While he acknowledged the fact that he was probably out of his depth, Henry was not a fool – certainly not the incompetent idiot with whom Crawford had compared him – so he could at least try to use his wits.

He got off the bed. "Come on now," he said with a contrived note of impatience, endeavouring to call their bluff, "this isn't good enough. Unless you get to the point, I'm going to call the police ... "

Neither man seemed particularly concerned. It seemed likely that the giant responded only on direct orders – but his companion remained seated, fastidiously examining his fingernails. He looked up suddenly, poker-faced, and replied, "By all means: there is a telephone along the passage. Hassan will not stop you."

Henry momentarily toyed with the idea of contacting Inspector Kahn, but if these men wanted to stop him they could, and in any case what accusation would he level against them? He sat down again on the bed, his stomach churning. Conscious that his face had lost its colour, he stopped trying to be clever and again demanded to know who they were.

His tormentor smiled. "I'm more interested in who *you* are, Mr Franklin ... ?"

Henry's surprise stemmed his anxiety. " ... Me? It seems you already know ... "

"Your name, perhaps, and your 'cover' story, but that is not very enlightening. You were working with Hamilton, but you are not part of D16?"

"Of course not. Despite what everyone chooses to believe, I am a librarian. It's easy enough to check!"

"We shall. It may be the truth – but still a cover. Most of the intelligence agencies use free-lances. Some of them more efficient and deadlier than their masters."

Henry's stare was incredulous. "Is that what you think I am?"

The question was answered by another. "You asked who we were? I could say that we were friends, but since we were responsible for shooting your friend Hamilton, I don't suppose it would sound very convincing. That is why I am intrigued by your real identity. In certain circumstances, we could still be friends ... "

"I'm still waiting to hear who *you* are ... ?"

"*Touché.* I was beginning to believe from your example that names do not matter, but as a matter of courtesy I will introduce myself. The name is Omar Rashid. My friend here, as you heard, is Hassan. No need to exchange pleasantries – he speaks only Urdu."

Henry shrugged. "As you said, names mean very little. What do you want with me?"

Rashid smiled. "Back to square one, Mr Franklin. If you are not prepared to meet me halfway ... cards on the table and all that ... then Hassan will make you co-operate, and that will not be very pleasant."

"There is nothing to tell," Henry protested. "I'm busy enough trying to cope with my job in the library, and a fiancée who thinks I'm not ambitious enough, without leading a double-life."

A shadow of anger crossed Rashid's face as he began to lose his composure. "Do not be patronizing, Mr Franklin. It was no ordinary librarian who helped Hamilton fight off the ruffians we hired to attack you; and the marksman who took him out with one shot reported that your reactions were like lightning!"

It was on the tip of Henry's tongue to point out that he had merely fainted, but he realized that Rashid would not be amused. "How did you know about my part in the fight? If they were local thugs I doubt whether they were capable of a coherent report. The only person who really knew – because Hamilton told him – was Colonel Crawford. He was also the only person who knew I was here."

Rashid seemed to relax. "If I expect you to be honest, I must be equally frank with you. It *was* that pompous idiot, Colonel Crawford, who told us these things – and the fact that you read and speak Arabic. Now, isn't that also a strange coincidence in the circumstances, Mr Librarian?"

Henry sensed there was little point in trying to conceal the truth, or becoming a martyr for the likes of Beckton. "There were some stolen manuscripts. My job was to ensure that they were genuine, so that Hamilton could buy them back."

"*Buy* them back?" Rashid laughed.

The penny dropped at last, and Henry realized why Beckton had not been interested in values. He said nothing.

"So you *are* a free-lance?" Rashid demanded.

Henry hesitated. If he persisted with the truth, it was unlikely that Rashid would believe him. He could lose nothing by going along with the subterfuge. "What difference does it make?" he asked.

Rashid nodded with approval at the apparent change of heart. "It changes things – possibly to our mutual advantage."

Henry raised a questioning eyebrow.

"Some of the best free-lances use their discretion, and work for more than one master. *We* need all the expertise we can get ... and there is no reason why you should not profit from the arrangement ... "

"Profit?"

"Financially. After all, my Cause is in no way a threat to the safety of your country, so it is not even a question of scruples."

"You said 'financially'?"

"Yes. We are not rich, but we can certainly match what the British Foreign Office pays ... "

Henry struggled to keep a straight face. If Rashid only knew the extent of his reward! "What happens if I choose not to accept your generosity?"

Rashid's eyes moved to the silent Hassan, and the implication was so obvious that Henry began to feel his composure slipping away again. He forced a smile, so stiff that he had difficulty in speaking clearly. "How do I know that you won't kill me anyway?"

"Why?" Rashid's expression registered surprise. "It is in our interest to have as many friends as possible. If you prove useful to us, what incentive is there for killing you?"

"Ensuring that I did not report back to D16 ... "

"Not so. Once you have helped us, you would have to think twice about your involvement when 'spilling the beans', as your American friends say. In any case, the chances are that what you had to tell them would be too little and too late. Nevertheless, if you did behave stupidly, we would have to punish you."

Henry nodded, indicating that he accepted the logic of Rashid's argument. "The only trouble is that I'm due to go back to England tomorrow, or the next day – as soon as my passport is returned."

Rashid's reaction was a hesitant smile, followed by a roar

of laughter. He said something to Hassan in Urdu and the giant also laughed. Since the proposition was such a huge joke, Henry cracked a smile to prove that he was a dry old stick.

Trapped, the only course open to him was to play for time, and pray that he would find a way to escape. Meanwhile, hoping to allay their suspicions even further he recalled the Foreign Office report on Arab revolutionary groups. The men with whom he was now involved were not Arabs, but certainly Muslims. "I saw a dossier on revolutionary groups in this area. I don't think there was more than a passing reference to you ... "

"I should hope so," said Rashid. "We are not the sort of people to court publicity. We do not go around throwing bombs in airports, or high-jacking planes. Most people will not know about us until our goals have been achieved. Perhaps when we get to know each other, I shall explain."

Henry tried to look enthusiastic. "It might surprise you to learn that I'm not unsympathetic. I studied Arab history and Islam at university, and I developed a *feeling* for many of the ideals that motivate you."

To his surprise, Rashid, after a moment's hesitation, deflected the olive branch. "For the time being, let us keep the relationship on a business footing. That way we know where we are. Meanwhile you have not given me your answer? Will you join us?"

Henry nodded, relieved it had been so easy to pull the wool over their eyes. It was just a question of using his brains, he reminded himself.

He was wrong again, of course.

Four

While he remained anxious over what might lie in store, Henry had to concede it was a relief to get away from the squalid lodging-house. Logic assured him that so long as his captors considered he was useful, he was in no immediate danger; it was probably no coincidence that after the initial handshake their attitudes changed, as though they were making a conscious effort to put him at his ease. When they left, Rashid was all smiles, and while Hassan still regarded him with detachment, there were encouraging little signs – such as an imperceptible bow before holding the car door open for him.

Henry got into the back seat of the inconspicuous black Citroën with Rashid, and they sat in silence until approaching the outskirts of the city. At a deserted spot on the winding coast road Hassan stopped, and Rashid announced somewhat apologetically that he would have to be blindfolded. He held out a clean silk scarf. "You may tie it yourself," he added.

The Englishman accepted the silk scarf philosophically, but could not help asking if it was customary to welcome new recruits with such apparent lack of trust?

Rashid chose to take him seriously. "You have yet to prove you can be trusted," he said, but his manner was conciliatory.

With the blindfold in place, Henry lost all sense of time and direction. At a rough guess the rest of the journey took a quarter of an hour, but at the end he had no idea of the location – he might have been back in the heart of the city – although he doubted that they would have driven through comparatively busy streets without some effort to conceal him and the conspicuous scarf. The car stopped on gravel, but it would have been foolish to place any significance on that, and with Rashid guiding him by a hand at his elbow, they entered a cool building. They had to walk up a flight of stone or marble stairs, and along a corridor before reaching the room where the blindfold was removed. Venetian blinds shaded the later afternoon sun, but even so Henry blinked painfully at the sudden explosion of light.

When his eyes had adjusted to the change he noticed there were three men sitting in the shadows, and a fourth in the centre of the room – his arms and legs tied to the hard wooden chair in which he sat. The man returned Henry's stare with glazed eyes, and the librarian began to feel what was now a familiar uneasiness in the pit of his stomach. The other three men were rather typical of young nationalists or guerrillas, and were even similar in appearance – from the cut of their hair to their expressions, ranging from pride to arrogance. They watched Henry warily but remained motionless as though awaiting orders, and Rashid, who was obviously in command, told Henry that he was about to learn something to his advantage.

Rashid turned to the prisoner, a middle-aged man with pleasantly regular features marred only by the dark shadows of his shaven head. His face glistened with perspiration and a muscle at the side of his mouth ticked nervously, but he tried to conceal his fear by keeping his eyes fixed straight ahead. He refused stubbornly to look at Rashid as the group's leader addressed him.

"Embarek Akhtar! You have been found guilty of betraying privileged information to the Government police. Have you anything to say before the sentence of this court is passed ... ?"

Stoically, Akhtar remained silent and Henry, despite an ingrained contempt for traitors, experienced a moment of admiration for the man. But at Rashid's next words, his sympathy turned to horror, and the hair at the back of his neck seemed to stand damply on end.

"The punishment for traitors in normal circumstances is death – but we must demonstrate to our visitor that we are merciful. You will have a punishment more fitting to your crime." He gestured to Hassan who had been standing in his customary position by the door.

As Hassan stepped forward, Henry searched for an opportunity to intercede on the prisoner's behalf. There was nothing he could do physically, but perhaps they might listen to reason ... Yet there was something in the manner of these men that grossly exceeded the bounds of duty. Hassan's face was an impassive mask; robot-like he was concerned only with the execution of Rashid's command. But the others, he noticed, seemed to be anticipating some move from him, and watched him like hawks. He wondered if the court had been staged to test his reactions.

From a cupboard in a corner of the bare, barrack-like room, Hassan took an ordinary table tennis bat, cheaply finished with cork and sandpaper sides instead of rubber. He walked over to Akhtar whose nerve was beginning to crack, now looking at him intently with a mixture of curiosity and fear on his sweating face. Without a word, Hassan raised the bat in his right hand and brought the flat side down with frightening force to the side of the prisoner's head. It connected with the loud hollow echoing noise of a pistol shot, stunning Akhtar but leaving him fully conscious.

His eyes filled with pain, and Henry looked on in horror at the trickle of blood which began to seep from the man's ear. Without need of further evidence he knew that Akhtar was irretrievably deaf in that ear. While the shock was still registering, Hassan dispassionately brought the bat down to the other side of Akhtar's face. This time the force was so great that he was knocked over, the chair grating harshly on the stone floor.

Henry moved forward involuntarily, but Hassan stepped in front of him and with one hand, effortlessly righted the chair and its occupant. Henry looked at the three guards and discovered they were still watching him; each with a hand in a jacket pocket from which a familiar bulge pointed ominously in his direction, as though they expected him to burst into action. Obviously his reputation had preceded him.

He listened dully as Rashid addressed the prisoner again: "No more listening at keyholes for you! Perhaps it is just as well you cannot hear the rest of the court's sentence – the punishment for a flapping tongue!" He looked over at Hassan, signalling him to proceed.

This time the giant stood behind the prisoner and forced open his jaws. From one of the guards, Omar Rashid accepted a pair of sugar tongs, and firmly grasped Akhtar's tongue. Ignoring the frantic appeal in the man's staring eyes, he took a long knife proffered to him and dispassionately cut it out.

While the nightmarish action was being enacted, Henry's own tongue seemed to swell up at the back of his throat. He had retained a slight hope that Rashid was bluffing, but as the blood spurted, his stomach tried to climb into his mouth. He had not eaten for several hours so there was no food to bring back, but he felt violently ill. His body was suddenly bathed in cold sweat, and he fought to overcome waves of blackness. He was conscious of them all looking at him, and his pride finally asserted itself. Weakly, he leaned against the wall and opened his eyes.

"The car journey has obviously upset your stomach," Rashid remarked. It was accompanied by a cold smile.

For a moment, Henry forgot his terror. "The journey – or the company I keep," he said with unconcealed loathing, getting courage from his spontaneous daring.

But Rashid shrugged indifferently. "You had to learn that the betrayal of a sacred trust must be punished," he said.

Significantly, when they left, the blindfold was not replaced, but Henry was too demoralized to take advantage of it. He looked straight ahead, but Hassan's thick neck only served to remind him of the unfortunate Akhtar. When he closed his eyes, the blackness merely brought the bloodstained face into sharper focus.

He was only vaguely aware of arriving at Rashid's destination, and being escorted into a villa he would not have been able to describe, except that it seemed cool and spotlessly clean. In a daze, he was taken to a bedroom and told to rest. Rashid was surprisingly considerate, giving him a bottle of aspirin. "Perhaps you have a virus," he suggested. Henry felt too ill to disagree and within five minutes he was asleep. He seemed to remember at one stage that it was sensible to unfasten his shoelaces, but he did not have time.

Henry slept for fifteen hours, and awoke feeling immeasurably better. It was nearly midday and he was pleased to see that a breakfast tray had been left on a dressing-table. The ice in the fresh orange juice had practically melted, but he was convinced that never in his life had he tasted anything so refreshing. It was an English-style breakfast of hard-boiled eggs, cheese and toast, with coffee sensibly left in a thermos flask, and Henry did not leave a crumb.

Rashid was apparently delighted at the transformation. "I thought you were going down with pneumonia, or one of these strains of Asian flu," he declared.

Henry suspected that the symptoms were more indicative of shock, but decided to say nothing. Having survived a whole day he was now sanguine about the utterly wrong impression they had of him. "Don't you think it is time to put me in the picture? At least, about what you have in store for me? Presumably, I am not here because you enjoy my company?"

"That is not so far from the truth as you imagine," Rashid protested. "I respect cultured men. But you are right, of course. Have you any idea why we wanted the manuscripts from England?"

Henry shook his head. "I was given no explanation, but it seems the truth can be interpreted in a variety of ways. I was told it was the work of a revolutionary group, but when I began to think about it, people like that would be the last to offer them back to us. Even if the motive was money, there must be rich private collectors who would have paid a much higher price than our impoverished libraries."

Rashid nodded appreciatively. "It was *not* the prime consideration, of course. In any case, all we intended to offer were a few which had identifiable library markings; as you know, most collectors are wary of buying stolen goods."

Henry suppressed a grin at Rashid's strange concept of moral values, but did not interrupt.

"Many of the treasures stolen from us originally to satisfy the greed of Western museums and libraries, are regarded as little more than works of art – admittedly of great antiquity, but pretty *baubles* nevertheless. Because Westerners are obsessed with this beauty, they are blind to far greater values in Islamic heritage ... "

"Such as your dream – Islam, the dominant force it once

was? Presumably, most of the manuscripts have a symbolic value ... a message ... ?"

"A message," Rashid echoed. "Admit it, Mr Franklin, what do your people care about the content of these old documents? They drool over the calligraphy, but they do not care a damn about the text."

Henry shrugged, unabashed. "That's true, but then it doesn't follow that those of us who *can* read are necessarily as easily impressed. In Western literature some of the most priceless books and manuscripts are 'curiosities', valued because of their uniqueness. In your culture some of the poetry and verse is magnificent, but the hymns of praise to Allah ... what I call 'dogma' ... are seldom anything out of the ordinary, and not very different to the preachings of today – stuffed with rhetoric."

Rashid smiled indulgently. "A politician would never dismiss rhetoric. He knows that lucid intellectual debate is wasted on the masses."

"I can understand your interest in that, but not in me ... unless it's something to do with the other material – your pretty 'baubles'. Perhaps you think I know some likely customer ... ?"

Rashid shook his head.

Despite his determination not to co-operate in whatever plan Rashid had in mind, Henry was curious. "So ... ?"

"You will accuse me of hypocrisy. Having talked of idealism, I have to admit that we cannot ignore financial considerations. Only a few kilometres away there is a museum which houses a truly great work of art – admittedly a bauble by the definition I used before, but one that is worth a king's ransom. At an auction in London some years ago the sale price was over sixty thousand pounds. It is worth much more today in the open market, and I know of two very rich men who would pay even more in a private auction – to prevent each other from possessing it.''

Henry was childishly reluctant to give Rashid the satisfaction of showing his growing curiosity. ''Doesn't ring a bell. It must be a richly decorated Koran?''

''Qur'an in this instance ... written in Baghdad by Yagut al-Musta'simi ... ''

''The Sultan of Calligraphers,'' Henry interrupted, ''thirteenth century ... '' He was impressed.

''Twelve eighty-two,'' Rashid corrected. ''I am told that some of the illumination is of the sixteenth and seventeenth centuries; but that these relatively modern embellishments have not affected the value.''

''The attraction lies in the scribe, not the additional material – beautiful though it is. I've seen a photograph.''

He was already trying to fathom out why Rashid needed him, when he was not short of men with far more experience of stealing. He tried to visualize himself shinning down a rope ladder from a skylight ... climbing up a drainpipe under the cover of darkness – but even as the pictures flashed through his subconscious, he knew he could never go through with anything like that. It was nothing to do with being scared at the prospect – and he certainly was – but even with a key to the door, he could not rob a library any more than take the contents of a blind man's tin mug. But there was no point in antagonizing Rashid, he reasoned; better to acquiesce for the present and somehow contrive to fail in the operation itself. If he was clever, Rashid need not suspect.

But he had underestimated the Pakistani again. Rashid did not see him in the role of cat burglar. ''The authorities keep the manuscript under lock and key, and have a facsimile realistic enough to fool most people, which they think is good enough to put on display,'' he explained. ''This is why we need you. They do show the real manuscript to a few people – scholars and those with a special interest, like yourself. My plan is that while you are studying it, my men will burst in and rob the place. It will be just a coincidence and no-one will suspect you were involved. You will give a statement to the authorities, and leave. From that moment your work for us is over, and you will be richer by five hundred pounds. We can part company, or – if you wish – continue the business association by selling the material we discussed before on a commission basis. It will be your decision."

Henry forced a smile. "Sounds straightforward enough ... " Even though he had no intention of carrying out Rashid's orders, he could not help feeling relieved that so little was required of him. Obviously one of the benefits, he reasoned, of being an expert; a consultant as opposed to a mere field operative.

But the glow of self-satisfaction was extinguished by Rashid's next remarks. "Of course, before we hand over that sort of money, we will have to be convinced you can be trusted ... "

"Convinced?" Henry's heart sank even lower.

"By another small operation for which there is no fee. It is only a *test* after all ... In fact you would not have to *do* anything – just tag along to make up the team ... get a 'feel' of the way we work."

"Team?"

"Just Hassan. Tomorrow he will put poison in part of the city's water supply ... "

"*Poison!*"

" ... and you will accompany him, in case he needs any assistance; really more to show us how you behave in these situations."

"You did say *poison!*"

Rashid raised a weary eyebrow at Henry's expression of

horror. "Relax, my friend. It's not what you think ... "

Henry was torn between relief that Rashid was not completely unbalanced, and fear that he was lying. "What *is* there to think? You haven't been exactly squeamish so far," he accused.

"Not by your hypocritical standards, perhaps. If I had to kill innocent people ... women and children, even ... to achieve something vital to the Cause, I would not hesitate. Fortunately, no such crisis exists. We do not intend to kill *anyone* for the moment."

Henry remained suspicious. "Poisoning the water supply is not dangerous?"

"Of course it is, but the operation has been planned with considerable care. If our calculations are correct – and I assure you, they *are* – the people there are likely to suffer from muscular cramp, sickness and diarrhoea for a few days – nothing worse."

"Then what is the point?"

"The point? ... well, when several thousand people are incapacitated by a strange sickness, an investigation will be ordered, and will uncover evidence of a CIA and Zionist plot ... "

"What evidence?"

"No need to concern yourself with the details."

"The police and security forces are not fools ... "

" ... I am not concerned with them," Rashid interjected. "There are millions of far more impressionable people out there. After one of our very effective whispering campaigns, they will not doubt for a moment that this is yet another example of Western imperialist treachery."

In a desperate effort to deter Rashid, Henry resorted to flattery. "It's ingenious. I'm impressed ... Pity you have to take such a gamble with people's lives ... *your* people ... "

Rashid was impatient. "I'm not interested in your

conscience, Mr Franklin, but since he happens to be here today I will introduce you to someone – an expert like yourself, but a research chemist." He snapped his fingers, and one of the young guards left the room and returned a few minutes later with a tall, untidy man looking as out-of-place in a shabby grey lounge suit as he probably felt. He acted as though he begrudged every minute spent away from his laboratory, nodding vaguely at Rashid and somewhat impatiently at Henry.

Rashid smiled at the newcomer, and without bothering with names, introduced him as the man who had produced the poison bacillus that Hassan would be using. He then asked the scientist to give Henry a brief description of the formula.

The man cleared his throat as though embarking on a lecture, and after glancing aggressively from one to the other, he began: "The name of this culture is *Clostridium botulinum* ... "

Henry shrugged, looking helplessly from the scientist to Rashid, and the stranger glared at him. "I regret your ignorance as much as you surely must. Perhaps you would rather I had reversed the procedure by selecting the simplest Latin name, and then deciding whether or not it is appropriate for our purpose!"

Rashid raised a soothing hand. "Please, Professor ... ! Our visitor meant no disrespect ... " The scientist looked sour but eventually continued: "My problem was to find a virus that was not too deadly, and yet not too mild when diluted in thousands of gallons of water. I experimented with several bacterium and finally decided on ... " He broke off and looked at Henry, who tactfully kept his eyes averted, before continuing, " ... which is a particularly virulent form of a rare bug of the type sometimes found in improperly canned foods. I already had this type of culture collection at my laboratory, so all I had to do was to grow some more in a broth form. Then to produce the liquid form we needed, I put it through a Seitz filter ... but you will not understand ... "

"Just as well," Henry retorted. "I'm sure it's brilliant, but I'm more concerned about a guarantee that it won't kill anyone."

The professor hesitated, although the reflection was on academic, not moral grounds. Eventually he added: "Without exhaustive tests, which are impractical in the circumstances, it is not possible to guarantee *anything*. But unless a person happens to be sick already ... "

Henry broke in cynically: "I wonder how many sick people there are in Karachi at this moment?"

Rashid put an end to the discussion which was not going the way he had expected. "We have already proved to our satisfaction that there is no undue risk to life."

Henry was wretched enough to risk a scowl of disbelief. He was surprised when Rashid bothered to respond.

"As a matter of fact," he said without heat, "the professor suggested that because of the vast quantity of water involved we would need a half-gallon of the stuff, but I preferred to err on the side of safety – quite apart from the fact that Hassan has to carry it." He pointed to what looked like a bottle of lemonade on a sideboard.

The 10-km car ride to the reservoir was a nightmare for Henry. If he had been able to communicate with Hassan, he would have attempted to dissuade him – in the faint hope that he had some spark of humanity – from going through with the operation. Instead, he would have to find a way of stopping him by other means. Concealed in an old rucksack, the bottle rested on the seat between them. Henry toyed with the idea of snatching it while Hassan was concentrating on the road ahead, and then hurling it out of the window. But even if the bottle smashed, his triumph would be short-lived – in the most sinister sense of the word. He would be merely postponing the inevitable, because Rashid would try again. Cautiously, he stared at the giant by his side. Hassan was probably not very intelligent – although even that was a wild assumption – but it would take someone of Hamilton's prowess to incapacitate him. His mind raced ahead searching for opportunities to catch him off guard.

Henry had been present at the final briefing; Rashid going over old ground for his benefit so that he was familiar with what was going on, should Hassan need help. Not wishing to confuse him with too much technical information, Rashid only gave a rough outline of the way water is collected, purified and distributed to the end-user. To kill ordinary bacteria, water is chlorinated by injection into the main pipe, but before it is drawn off by domestic requirement, it has to be de-chlorinated. It was at this pure stage that Hassan would be adding the contents of the lemonade bottle.

Rashid compared the system of distribution with the blood circulatory system – heavy fuel oil pumps doing the work of the heart, pushing out a continuous supply of the pure water along a main pipe (the arterial flow) from which subsidiary pipes (the ordinary blood vessels) drew off the amount needed in the course of a day. At the end of the main pipe was a storage reservoir which acts as a safety valve, accepting the surplus when requirement is low, and making up the balance when the pumps cannot meet excessive demands. This was their destination. Somewhere before that reservoir Henry had to come up with a ploy good enough to allow for the odds stacked against him physically.

Rashid had planned the operation for a Friday –

corresponding to the Christian Sunday – because in the afternoon there was only a skeleton staff on duty. In fact, when they arrived, the main gates were closed and Hassan decided to drive around the perimeter wall. He stopped at a deserted spot and glanced at the wall. Although he said nothing it was obvious that he was estimating its height and taking note of the tangle of barbed wire laid along the top.

From the front of the Citroën he took the two rubber mats, and using the bonnet as a platform, climbed up and draped them over the wire about four metres from the ground. Then, as though he had only just remembered his companion, he gestured Henry to climb up. Henry obeyed with resignation. He found that from the car roof he could reach the top of the mats with his outstretched fingers; it needed only a slight leap to get a firm grip and haul himself up. The soil on the other side was sandy so he had no fear of the drop. A few seconds later Hassan joined him and took the lead again, heading towards the building nearest the main gates.

The waterworks covered several acres and as they moved closer, the horizon seemed to be full of vast sheds and towers. Without a plan of the place, Henry quickly lost his sense of direction, but the giant knew where he was going. When they reached their destination he paused, put a finger to his lips as a warning and then crept inside. Henry heard the sound of a brief scuffle and when he followed, saw the gatekeeper unconscious on the floor. Scorning his help Hassan was already tying him up and gagging him. When he completed his task, Hassan used a metal chair to smash the telephone switchboard, before pulling it away from its fittings on the wall.

Henry was aghast at the mess. The tiny room looked as though it had been caught in the path of a hurricane, but he was relieved to see that the injured man was breathing quite

steadily. The doubts about his ability to stop Hassan were
suddenly magnified; the giant was like an indestructible
robot. The place seemed so quiet that he guessed they could
have carried out their plan without bothering about the
gatekeeper, but apparently Hassan was not a man to take
chances. Henry did not have time to dwell on his
inadequacy because Hassan was off again and he was
obliged to follow wherever the rucksack took him.

Confused by the array of buildings, despite Rashid's
careful explanation, Henry scampered after his companion.
They entered what looked like a huge circular black house
with a flat roof – which might have been attractively modern
in shape but for a shed-like door at the base, and two tiny
square windows almost lost high up in the structure. Hassan
sorted through the bunch of keys he had removed from the
gatekeeper, and selected a few likely ones. The bolt on the
door was so primitive Henry reckoned he could have
opened it with a piece of bent wire, but the keys were
preferred and it opened at the second attempt.

Inside they found a short wooden staircase leading to a
metal grilled platform which ran round the sides of the
building, and which overlooked a pool. The roof, which in
this hot climate maintained the water at an even
temperature and prevented evaporation, cleared their heads
by not more than six inches, and was so vast and oppressive
that Henry instinctively ducked his head after every few
strides. The total circumference was not so large, but,
constructed entirely in concrete – even the roof of flat
reinforced concrete slabs across concrete encased steel
beams – it created an atmosphere of awesome power.
Whatever it was, Henry felt frail and insignificant as he
peered down into the deep underground pool. Coupled
with the iron guard-rail less than waist high, the roof
appearing to bear down on his head, made him feel giddy

and for a moment he swayed. As he fought to pull himself together, he became aware of Hassan looking in his direction. Surprisingly, the giant who had been taking the bottle from the rucksack, stopped and came over to investigate.

At that stage Henry had no idea of how he might exploit the situation but instinct told him to maintain the charade. He swayed again, closed his eyes, and slumped to his knees. A moment later he was aware that the lemonade bottle had been placed between them so that Hassan could use both hands to help him to his feet. Without stopping to think of the risk he was taking, Henry hurled his full weight against Hassan's knees, catching the giant off-balance. Toppling backwards, Hassan's hips collided with the guard-rail, and he overbalanced into the water with a loud splash.

For Henry the relief was enormous and he was tempted to utter a cry of victory, or do a lap of honour round the platform, but he forced himself to stay calm. Priority was the bottle and he took a firm grip of it. But before he had reached the top of the stairs he was stopped in his tracks by panic-stricken cries from the pool. It was the first time he had heard Hassan make a sound of any sort, and now – since apparently he could not swim – there was a particularly weird note about it. He hesitated. Hassan was a cold-blooded killer over whom he should not lose any sleep – but drowning is a particularly unpleasant way to die, and he knew he would hear those screams for the rest of his life.

Dropping the bottle down the steps and hearing it smash out of harm's way, was something of a consolation as he retraced his steps. Cursing himself for his weakness he concentrated on finding a way to rescue the drowning giant. Luckily, the danger of someone falling in the water had been recognized, and there was a lifebelt on the wall nearby. Hassan's cries for help were now punctuated by fits of spluttering and choking. Henry could see him only a few feet below the platform, splashing about in a frantic and ineffective dog-paddle. He called out and the giant looked up, his eyes wild, almost unseeing. Henry indicated the lifebelt, miming his instructions in slow motion before dropping it carefully so it landed only a few inches from the drowning man's face.

Whether Hassan was not as desperate as he looked, or whether Henry's instructions had been impossible to misunderstand, he had no difficulty in grabbing the life-belt and slipping it under his arms. Henry tied one end of the attached rope to the guard-rail, and wrapped some of the slack around his body. Then he leaned back in tug-of-war style, and began to heave on the rope as though his life depended on it.

The water trapped in Hassan's clothing added to his considerable weight, but the guard-rail took most of the strain, and gradually he was inched up out of the pool. When his arms were level with the platform he was able to support himself, and Henry hurried over to help him back on to dry ground. At last Hassan lay on his side in near exhaustion, alternately spewing water and gasping for breath. Henry was uncertain what his next step should be. If it was too much to expect Hassan to believe that his fall had been an accident, or even to appreciate that Henry had rescued him, he hoped that the latter might at least make him a little more receptive to reason – perhaps even to turn a blind eye to Henry escaping.

While Hassan sat up, Henry still hovered nervously, wondering if there was still time to run, but hoping against hope that the worst was over. His brain was clogged with conflicting advice, and he recalled Hamilton's warning: " ... when in doubt, trust no-one ... " but while he hesitated, a massive hand grabbed his ankle in a vice-like grip. He tried to turn round and kick his assailant but he could not get the right leverage. The next thing he knew was that he had been up-ended and hurled along the platform.

Henry landed heavily on his shoulder, bruised by the impact but grateful that no bones appeared to have been broken. But as he got to his feet, Hassan hauled him by his jacket on to the tips of his toes. Henry tried a few punches but his timing was wrong and most of the blows landed ineffectually behind the giant's head. Hassan ignored these fruitless attempts to stop him and changed his grip, taking the jacket collar in one hand and the seat of his trousers in the other.

Henry was hoisted into the air, and from his position ten feet above the platform he tried to work out which was the least alarming feat – a head-on confrontation with the iron grating, or the water from which, for him, there could be no escape. Forlornly he struggled in the giant's grip, and more by luck than judgement the toe of one of his shoes caught Hassan on the ear. It was a sensitive spot and Hassan cried out. Imperceptibly he loosened his grip and Henry redoubled his efforts to land another blow on the same target. He was lucky and felt himself dropped like a sack of potatoes as Hassan clutched at his ear. The fall added to Henry's bruises, but this time desperation brought him to his feet with the agility of a cat, and in almost the same movement he was heading for the stairs.

He took the steps three at a time, reaching the bottom before Hassan had started in pursuit. He had reached the door of the shed when the first bullet missed by only inches. Henry fancied his chances of outsprinting Hassan to get to the car, despite the high wall in between, but there was no protection out in the open if Hassan continued to use his gun. Instead, he dashed into the nearest building in the hope that it was big enough to provide a few hiding-places.

It turned out to be the pumping-shed, about 100 feet long. The three pumps occupying the centre were like static traction engines, and they made as much noise, but there were plenty of shadows and Hassan might have problems finding him. There were also doors at either end of the shed, and another in the centre, although that appeared to be locked and bolted.

Still no sign of Hassan and Henry suspected he was waiting outside, believing that his prey was trapped! Realizing he would have to come out eventually, and that the two doors might be overlooked from one vantage position, he started searching for another way out. Within a few minutes he found a circular iron staircase leading down to the basement. It occurred to him that there was possibly an underground tunnel which might put a real distance between him and his pursuer. Following the hunch, he crept down into the basement where the heat immediately told him something that should have registered earlier – the pumps were furnace fed. The heat and noise were overpowering although he was too concerned with finding a way out to let it worry him. But after skirting the basement perimeter, all he could find was another matching staircase.

Cursing himself for his lack of foresight he had no option but to go upstairs again – and it was there that he met Hassan coming down. The giant's triumphant smile was like salt in the wound. No physical match for the Pakistani, Henry had been almost patronizing in his conviction that he could at least outwit him. Now he would have to pay the consequences.

He retraced his footsteps, eyes fixed on the gun pointing at his chest. Signalling him to stop by one of the furnaces, Hassan paused to open the coke door. The handle was swathed in asbestos so that he was able to grip it firmly with one hand as he ducked to one side to avoid the blast of hot air. Then, as the Pakistani took aim, Henry realized what was in store. He had always thought cremation was a sensible way to go, but not like this ... not here ... not yet ...

His ear drums reverberated at the sound of the shot, but mercifully felt no pain. Then to his surprise Hassan was on the ground, and there was blood seeping through his jacket at the back. Henry was dazed. The glare of the open oven made it difficult to see very far into the gloom beyond, but gradually his eyes made out a figure approaching, and in front of it another gun. Having come so close to death, Henry was too numb to feel apprehensive any more. But as the figure came into focus the butterflies returned – not because he was frightened, but because the newcomer was a woman so stunningly lovely that he knew he was in danger of losing his heart.

Five

She was quite tall – the top of her head was level with his chin, making her about five feet eight inches – and she moved with the flowing grace of a gymnast. Functional blue denim jeans and matching linen shirt were evidence that she did not dress for effect, yet with the shirt unbuttoned almost to the waist she might have stepped straight from one of the glamorous apéritif TV commercials. From her businesslike expression Henry could see she was unaware of the effect on him; the shirt was merely unbuttoned because of the heat – her face, throat and exposed chest glistening with perspiration.

Henry was suddenly conscious that his own clothes were sticking to him uncomfortably. The dry heat of the basement was fiercely oppressive, but until now he had been too preoccupied with Hassan to notice.

In the fraught circumstances, the girl had seemed to materialize like an apparition, a lovely vision – an avenging angel. Inevitably, on closer inspection she fell short of such perfection. There were minor flaws – her forehead was fractionally too wide and her eyes imperceptibly too far apart – yet by earthy standards of beauty, they added an extra dimension, the strength of character. The remarkable face, devoid of make-up, was framed by a cascading mass of blonde hair reaching to the nape of her neck; her eyes were a dark blue and the lips full and naturally red. Whoever was responsible for the assembly of such a mixed assortment of genes had done a sensational job.

Henry was mesmerized. He had an aesthetic appreciation of beauty, but it was not enough in itself and he looked for other qualities. This irresistible combination of beauty and brains was unique; the girl being as ruthless and efficient as the giant she had destroyed. He was suddenly desperately anxious to show himself worthy of her concern, to impress her. First impressions were important. She had saved his life; he needed to respond with *savoir faire*, with words that were not only appropriate but witty and laid-back.

Inspired phrases flashed through his brain, jostling for attention, but even as he tried to sift them, he could hear his voice feebly echoing his subconscious: "I don't know who you are, Miss, but you saved my life!" The words tumbled out before he could bite his tongue, and he was left to curse his inadequacy. *How cool!*

As it happened, recriminations were pointless because the girl did not seem to hear him. "Who are you?" she demanded, before he had finished speaking.

Her English was good, but there was a faint guttural quality that sounded middle European. There was also an undertone of suspicion, reminding him it was not the time for introspection, let alone light-hearted banter.

"My name is Henry Franklin. Who are *you?*"

The revolver pointed at his chest did not waver. "British or American? D16? CIA?"

He shrugged. "Neither, I'm afraid ... " He was on the point of speaking the truth, but an unfamiliar sense of bravado overwhelmed his scruples. He was tired of being honest, only to discover that people out here did not believe him anyway. Everyone seemed to be convinced that he was an undercover agent, so there could be little harm in going along with the idea. "Let's just say I'm freelance," he remarked.

"With D16?"

A direct lie was too risky in the circumstances. He gave the answer that she might have expected. "You know I can't talk about things like that – at least, not before we have been properly introduced."

She shrugged. "Please yourself." The gun was lowered, and she turned to leave.

Henry panicked at the prospect of losing her. "Wait a minute! I can't let you go just like that! If you hadn't turned up I would have been fuelling these pumps by now. I don't even know who you are … ?"

"No problem – it is of no consequence," she said, heading for the staircase.

Desperation restored life to his legs and he hurried after her. At the foot of the staircase, his hand at her shoulder caused her to whirl round instinctively, the nozzle of the gun instantly level with his forehead. To his surprise, Henry was no longer scared by guns. He sensed it was a reflex action, and that she had not needed to wait until now to shoot him.

"I said 'wait'. What's the hurry? Perhaps we can help each other? I owe you a favour, at least."

She lowered the gun. "I make my own luck. I do not need favours. My job was to prevent them poisoning the water. Technically it was over the moment you smashed the bottle."

"Then why did you stay?"

"I don't always stick to the rule book. I recognized the big guy as one of them, so when he tried to kill you, I decided to stop him … "

"Which is why I'm grovelling at your feet at this moment!"

"No need to grovel! It may have been your lucky day, but

I'm afraid my intention was to eliminate an enemy – not to save you."

"What happens if his people try again?"

"What do *you* know about his people?"

"Not much, but probably things you don't know. Why don't we compare notes?"

"Why should I trust you? A moment ago you refused to identify yourself ... "

"I told you my name!"

"What is a name? I am more concerned with what you *are*," she said contemptuously.

"Well, it's more than you told me ... "

"My name is Ruti Kenan ... "

"Ruti ... ?"

"I was given the name Ruth, but my friends call me ... "

He clutched at straws, inferring what he wanted to infer. "Thanks."

She returned his smile. "I suppose you will now say that friends should have no secrets from each other?"

"If it means being friends with you, I'll admit whatever you like – even that I'm with D16. Actually, two of us flew over from London, but my partner was shot."

Her smile evaporated. "We heard that an Englishman was killed, but it has been difficult to get the facts. The police are very cagey."

" 'We' being Mossad – Israeli Intelligence?"

She ignored his stab in the dark, answering it with a question of her own. "You were both working undercover?"

He nodded. "It's a bit more complex than that, but the basic idea was to infiltrate their organization. To test my loyalty they forced me to go to the waterworks but I couldn't go through with it. How did *you* know there was poison in that bottle?"

"An informer, what else? Some of these people would sell their own mothers for money."

Henry recalled the young men surrounding Rashid, and perhaps naîvely gave them credit for being a cut above bribery. The impatient scientist was a more likely candidate, but he offered no opinion, knowing that she would not confide in him. "Let's get out of this heat," he suggested.

She gestured towards the body of Hassan. "You may as well take the gun. It's a Beretta, a fine revolver." Misunderstanding his hesitation, she added sarcastically: "You English are so conventional! It may not be standard issue, but I assure you it works ... "

He resisted his instinctive desire to leave it and ignore her advice; if he was playing a role he would have to act in character. "I must admit I miss my Luger," he lied. "They promised they would return it after the job, but I don't think I shall risk going back for it."

"It would be suicide," she agreed, adding more sympathetically, "don't worry. I once used a Beretta. I liked it."

Henry wondered about the significance of that remark. Much as he hated to admit it, it would be difficult to live up to her expectations. His eyes focussed on the gun only inches away from Hassan's lifeless hand. *So that's what it is? A Beretta?* Under her watchful gaze he had no alternative but to retrieve it. He did not attempt to unstrap the shoulder holster Hassan had been wearing; he had no intention of using the weapon so he was only going through the motions for the sake of appearances.

Following Ruti upstairs, he wondered how he was going to escape Rashid's wrath; whether he should go straight to police headquarters and tell Inspector Khan the whole story, or whether he would be safe for a while at the Balimar. His apparent indecision about going back for his gun had been a mixture of bluff and bravado, but there was no harm in taking the time to work out a plausible story in case Rashid caught up with him.

Outside the shed he was rather surprised to find the waterworks were still deserted. It seemed he had been inside for hours, time enough for the next shift to come on duty but a glance at his watch indicated that little more than an hour had passed. He followed the girl instinctively, confident that she knew what she was doing. With Hassan on his heels, the prospect of scaling a twelve-foot wall had not seemed at all unreasonable, but without the adrenalin that only panic could provide, it was far more daunting. Fortunately his instinct did not let him down; it transpired that the same girl had followed them, and climbed the wall at the same spot, although she had used a grappling hook and rope, which now provided their escape route.

On the other side of the wall was a second car – a little red Fiat looking bright and perky alongside Hassan's sombre Citroën, until Henry realized that the contrast was accentuated by the fact that the air had been let out of the bigger car's tyres. His confusion was offset by the knowledge that she intended giving him a lift to town; and if he was with her he could hardly ask to be dropped off at police headquarters.

As they got into the car, she asked if he had a safe address.

He told her where he was staying and put the same question to her.

The girl hesitated, but while she was studying the street map, her finger stabbed at a spot on the M.A. Jinnah road about a mile from the Balimar. "I have a flat there, but for now it is not convenient for you to come," she said withdrawing her finger quickly, as though regretting her impulsive breach of secrecy.

The incident served to remind Henry that they were

playing charades; that in reality they had nothing in common, and that they came from very different worlds. Yet that did not make it any less exciting. For the first time in his life he was being handed an opportunity to act out his fantasies. To refuse meant that he would lose the girl, an integral part of it.

"I thought we were going to compare notes?" he asked.

She started the car and headed back to Karachi. "I am not sure it is a good idea. It is true we have certain common interests, but our ultimate objectives may well conflict. I do not think my superiors would be very keen on the idea – or yours."

He wondered which of his superiors she might mean?

He thought instinctively of Arthur Hardcastle, chairman of the Finance Committee, and grimaced. Even Beckton's face was discouraging. "You're probably right," he conceded, "but we're human beings, not machines. I know this is not exactly a holiday, but even if we are on call twenty-four hours a day, we have to eat and sleep. I suppose it's presumptuous to talk of sharing a bed, but at least we can have a meal together."

Surprised, she took her eyes off the road to check that he was not pulling her leg. Then when she smiled at his boldness, his stomach flipped. He was even tempted to lean over and kiss her, but his natural caution prevailed – he did not know how she would react and the last thing they needed at this moment was to get involved in a road accident. He restricted himself to a plaintive, "Well?"

She smiled again. "I do need to eat. If you are staying at the hotel, perhaps I shall telephone you there ... "

It was vague, but as much as he could expect without making himself look ridiculous.

Inspector Khan sounded relieved but curious on the

telephone. "Where have you been, Mr Franklin? We have been concerned ... "

"I'm fine, Inspector. Any news of my passport?"

"I have it on my desk. You may leave whenever you wish."

Henry felt a mixture of relief and disappointment at the unwelcome reminder that his dreams of a future with the Israeli girl were divorced from reality. He suppressed a sigh. "I'll go to the airline offices tomorrow as soon as they open, although I might stay on for another day or so," he said. "As you pointed out, having come so far it's a pity to rush back without seeing anything. Is it necessary for me to collect the passport in person?"

"I shall drop it round myself this evening on my way home," Khan replied.

The Balimar had kept his room, but his personal possessions at Rashid's villa were irretrievably lost; it was hardly politic to seek their return. Fortunately he still had money and travellers' cheques, so that he could at least buy anything he needed. It had turned out to be an unexpectedly expensive visit, and he wondered if Beckton could be induced to compensate him.

Henry was enjoying an evening meal in the restaurant when Khan arrived and joined him for coffee. The inspector was outwardly as relaxed and friendly as before, but Henry was conscious of an undercurrent of reserve, as though – despite the clean bill of health arising from the enquiries in England, the inspector's own suspicions had not been completely removed. After the exchange of pleasantries, he again asked where Henry had been. "I checked with your embassy, but they were as surprised as us by your disappearance."

"Disappearance? It didn't occur to me that anyone might jump to that sort of conclusion," Henry said. "I'm sorry if

I've put you to any bother. I just needed a change of scenery for a couple of days. It had been quite an unnerving experience."

Khan did not seem to be listening. "Where did you go?"

Henry forced a laugh. "Haven't I wasted enough of your time, Inspector? I'm back now ... hopefully out of your hair for good."

Khan shrugged. "Please don't let that concern you. I'm paid to ... " His voice trailed off and when Henry raised a questioning eyebrow, he added, "I was going to say 'protect the innocent', but ... "

" ... But you're not sure whether the cap fits; if I am as innocent as I appear?"

The inspector smiled. "It is a question of loose ends. I have a tidy mind."

"What loose ends?"

"Do you remember I promised we would keep an eye on you if you stayed at the hotel? In the circumstances we were surprised when you decided to take a taxi, with what appeared to be an overnight case. One of my men followed you. He was even more bewildered by the type of place you decided to stay at, so we kept it under surveillance until you were collected by a couple of strangers. Somehow our people managed to lose you, but we were able to trace the car's registration number. Perhaps you would complete the story?"

It was pointless trying to maintain his innocent act, and Henry decided it was safe to reveal part of the story. "I was the guest of a man called Omar Rashid ... " He was conscious of Khan's encouraging nod, but the policeman did not interrupt. "Since the number plate was traced, you may already know that. I have no idea what else you know, but for what it's worth, Rashid is the leader of a fanatical Islamic sect ... "

" ... We know Mr Rashid," Khan interjected.

Henry remembered the unfortunate Akhtar but thought it prudent not to mention the informer's fate. "His activities don't worry you?"

"They worry me, of course, but I am a policeman. I can do nothing unless these people break the law, and we can catch them in the act ... "

"For what it is worth, Rashid admitted that it was his men who killed Mr Hamilton."

"Unless he presented you with a signed confession, preferably witnessed, it is a more difficult matter to prove it. But I am fascinated by Mr Rashid's interest in you. I take it that the word 'guest' can be attributed to the British sense of humour?"

Henry decided to embroider the facts with the partial truth about the theft of Arabic manuscripts. When he had completed his account, he added: "He promised to reward me handsomely if I would collaborate with them ... "

"Collaborate?"

"Authenticate them where necessary; in some cases help find buyers. His is also talking about robbing museums of their prize possession. I told him it was out of the question. I am a librarian ... "

" ... So you keep reminding me."

" ... not a fence for stolen property."

"So he apologized for troubling you, and just let you go?" Khan's tone was heavy with sarcasm.

Henry felt himself flushing. "You didn't let me finish. I did realize, of course, that I might not have a choice, so I let it appear that I was responsive to persuasion. He kept raising the sum of money involved, and I admitted that I was tempted. After all, one doesn't earn a fortune as a ... "

" ... as a librarian?"

Henry ignored the jibe. "I said it was a big step and that I would have to think about it."

"And *then* he let you go?" Khan was still far from convinced.

"He knew that my passport had been confiscated – which meant that I couldn't run away. They said they would wait forty-eight hours for my decision; that was when they mentioned Mr Hamilton – to scare me."

"And you were scared?"

"Of course."

"Enough to do as they asked?"

"Of course *not*."

"But not enough to come straight to me?"

"I didn't think anyone would believe me. If we had confronted him, it would have been my word against his. He could deny we had ever met ... what could I prove?"

"So what *did* you intend to do?"

"Assuming my passport was returned – to go back to England. It was my safest bet."

"After you had done a little sightseeing?"

"I reckoned I would be safe within his time limit, and that it might look more natural if I appeared to carry on as normal."

Khan's attitude had changed imperceptibly, as though he might be giving Henry the benefit of the doubt. "The situation has changed now," he remarked.

"Oh? How is that?"

"Having been put in the picture I am obliged to offer you some sort of discreet protection ... "

"I wouldn't say no to that!"

"Especially if you would consider helping us more positively ... "

"Such as?"

"As I said before, if we can actually catch them ... "

Henry anticipated the request. "No. It's too much to

ask," he interjected, thinking of Akhtar. "I'm a librarian!"

"Even if I believe that, I don't see what it has to do with it. Do you think it right that people like Rashid can raise two fingers at the law?"

"No, but ... "

"Obviously, I cannot *make* you co-operate. Even if you were not a foreigner ... "

"I would if I could, but ... "

"But you are frightened?"

"Yes."

Khan shrugged. For the first time there was an element of sympathy in his manner. "*That* I can believe," he said.

Henry felt inadequate, wishing there was some way in which he could help. "Who is this Rashid?" he asked, conscious of an awkward silence. "I mean, where does he get his backing?"

"I wish we knew," Khan admitted. "He has quite a reputation as the editor of an English language political newspaper. Very right wing, but respectable. With advertising, it just about pays for itself – certainly not enough to buy that villa, or provide for the dozen or so young men he usually has in attendance. There has to be another source. Why do you ask?"

"Just curious. Presumably they're not above raising funds illegally; the stolen manuscripts, for example."

Nodding, the inspector got up to leave. "Thank you again, Mr Franklin. My men will keep an eye on the place. Here is my card – if anything else occurs to you, please call. If I am not there a message will be relayed to me at once."

They shook hands and Khan left. Henry felt sorry for him – restricted by the law, ironically from competing on equal terms in a struggle in which men like Rashid and Hassan, Beckton and Hamilton would always have the edge. But it was not Henry's fight, and he was better out of it. The awareness caused him to change his mind about staying on for another day or so. He decided to get the first available flight home – but hardly had the decision been taken when the telephone rang. The caller was Ruti Kenan.

"Henry?" Her voice was as exciting as he remembered. "Will you have lunch with me tomorrow?"

In that split-second his priorities had changed again. He swallowed hard. "Of course."

"Good! I will collect you at midday." The receiver was replaced, before he could prolong the conversation. So much for getting out while the going was good!

Six

Ruti Kenan spotted him through the floor-to-ceiling tinted window of the hotel foyer, and waved exuberantly as though she was genuinely pleased to see him. Conscious of envious glances from the men clustered about the entrance, Henry could not resist puffing out his chest a little. Eye-catching in a flared, multi-coloured skirt and sleeveless yellow tee-shirt, she made even the vivid little Fiat look washed-out.

The knowledge that lunch together had been this beautiful girl's idea did wonders for Henry's self-esteem. For a change, he felt on top of the situation, no longer having to imitate John Hamilton – and as he passed the now familiar face of the man who had been hanging about most of the morning, he gave a confident wink, reasonably certain he was communicating with one of Khan's men, and even that side of it was under control. Startled, the man jumped imperceptibly but offered no comment or sign of recognition, although a few minutes later when Henry climbed into the Fiat he noticed the same man hurrying to another car parked nearby.

Ruti greeted him with a wide smile; a happy-go-lucky girl who might have been an old friend, and he was relieved that his persistence had paid off. "How long have you got?" he asked, greedy for every moment she conceded.

"A couple of hours."

"Pity. I thought we might go for a swim. I'm told the beaches are pretty empty."

"Another time, perhaps."

It was a depressing thought that there might not be another if he still intended leaving in the next day or so, but the awareness triggered off another possibility. "Have you ever been to England?"

She nodded. "For a holiday – with my parents when I was a girl. We spent some of the time in London, but I remember falling in love with Scotland." She smiled wistfully at the memory and he could not take his eyes away from the lovely profile.

He wondered about her age. Relaxed, she seemed much younger. He settled for something less personal. "How long have you been here?"

"Just over a month. Why do you ask?"

"You seem to be very much at home in Karachi."

She gave a hollow laugh. "I feel a long way from home."

"I meant that you seem to know your way about." He noted a road sign indicating that they were heading towards the university and the airport, and added: "*Now*, for example … I wouldn't know where to take you for lunch in the city centre, let alone on the outskirts."

He attributed her frown to the way the car in front was hogging the crown of the road. "As a matter of fact, I have not been to this restaurant before," she conceded. "It was recommended. I hope you like it."

The words were still fresh in his memory a few minutes later when, pulling out of a narrow side street into the main thoroughfare he had a premonition that she was going to stop at an unprepossessing café on the opposite corner. The street, Amir Khusro, was nondescript but the restaurant seemed little more than a large working man's café, with no visible doors, so that the wooden tables and chairs, and pin-table machines crammed in vacant spots could be seen clearly from outside. He could not believe they were actually going to eat here; anything less like the popular concept of a romantic rendezvous was difficult to imagine. He had heard that Israelis were down-to-earth, but he was disappointed that she seemed so insensitive about the occasion – unless, not having been here before, she was as surprised as him. He glanced at her quickly, but her expression had not changed.

The name of the place was almost impossible to decipher; a weighty coating of grime from the elements covering the original brown paint. He prayed she would not stop, but when the inevitable happened, he was too polite to question the decision. When they entered he noticed the walls were of the same neutral colour, and it was only the size of the place – there must have been over thirty tables – that gave it a token aura of respectability, only a slight cut above other shabby run-down cafés on the city fringe. An encouraging sign was that there was a sprinkling of Europeans in the place. It might have been because it was cheap, but he preferred to believe that it was because they knew where one found the best 'native' food – that they too had been recommended.

The atmosphere in the restaurant was quite humid, yet Ruti selected a table away from the only breeze coming from the wide openings on to the street – apparently preferring to rely on a huge old-fashioned electric fan suspended from the ceiling. There were three or four waiters, but they were immediately approached by a man he guessed was the proprietor, a tough-looking stocky individual, obviously capable of acting as his own 'bouncer' on occasion. The man's dark-skinned face was wreathed in smiles as he wiped muscular hands and forearms on a grubby apron tied round his middle, as though acknowledging the honour they were paying his humble establishment. He bowed with surprising courtesy towards Ruti and greeted them in good English.

Henry, wondering if public health inspectors covered this part of the city, could happily have dispensed with food and settled for a black coffee, but Ruti asked for a menu and he was obliged to examine it. There were only half-a-dozen dishes – none of which seemed to be very appetizing – but he forced himself to be optimistic, assuming that the cook sacrificed variety for quality, which was a feature of one of his favourite restaurants in London. While he hesitated, he ordered an iced lager, and a Campari and soda for Ruti.

His taste in food was conservative even in normal circumstances, so Henry would have preferred a 'safe' omelette and chips, or even a steak – except that he suspected it would probably turn out to be crocodile. But he had to put on an act if he expected to convince he was as cosmopolitan as her. "Why don't you decide?" he suggested. "You said the place was recommended. Besides, after a month, you must know a bit more about the local food than me."

She shrugged. "I am not an expert, but I know enough to go where the locals go whenever possible. At your hotel they probably serve roast beef and cabbage because they think that is what the English tourist wants … "

He was enchanted by the way she rolled her 'r's as in "rrrosbif" distracting him from his worries.

" … How do you like curry?" she asked.

"I can take it – or leave it," he said stoically, despite a sinking heart.

"Perhaps not," she decided, letting him off the hook. "I am quite used to highly spiced food, but you should be careful – unless you eat it a lot at home?"

Henry forced a laugh. "Perhaps we should settle for a cheese sandwich?"

"No need for that." Ruti looked up to catch the proprietor's eye. She gave the order in a near whisper, so that Henry was unable to hear. The man nodded at her respectfully, but his smile at the Englishman was puzzling. Henry looked at her questioningly, but the girl was equally mysterious. "It's a surprise," she said.

He smiled to conceal his discomfiture, but she seemed to read his thoughts.

"I'm not going to poison you. It would have been simpler to put a bullet into you yesterday."

He tried to meet her light-heartedness halfway. "How do I know you weren't running short of bullets?"

"The owner was smiling because what I ordered should really be eaten with the fingers. No offence, but you don't look the type. I can ask for cutlery if you insist ... ?"

Henry shrugged. "No thanks. When in Rome and all that ... " She looked puzzled by the expression, and beginning to feel queasy at the food in prospect he tried to change the subject. "Tell me about yourself? How long have you been in the job?"

"A few years."

"How did you get into it?"

She pulled a face. "It is very boring."

"Not at all. I'm interested. Go on, it can't be a state secret."

"Certainly not that," she conceded. "I studied Arabic at university."

"Snap."

"Snap?"

"It means – so did I."

"Oh. Is that why you were recruited?"

Henry laughed. "Arabic doesn't have quite the same significance in my country."

She seemed to share his amusement. "You would not

think so in my case either – I have never been sent to an Arab-speaking country. Languages was merely one of the disciplines that drew me to their attention."

"But isn't that typical of the convoluted thinking that seems to be needed to run any security operation?"

"Convoluted?"

" … Twisted. A man is a good chess player so send him to Russia because *everyone* plays chess and he won't be spotted by the KGB … "

He doubted if the girl grasped what he was struggling to explain because her attention was evidently beginning to wander. She seemed to be more interested in the other diners than in him. Hoping to recapture her interest, he asked where she lived in Israel, adding: "As a matter of fact I've often considered going … " He stopped, realizing that she was simply not listening. He paused for more than a minute but she did not seem to notice, convincing him that his instincts were correct. Her gaze moved about the room so restlessly that he might not have been there.

He was hurt, but determined not to give up. Although he was not hungry he used the delay in the arrival of their food as an excuse for heavy-handed humour. "I don't know which wild animal you ordered, but it looks as though they are having problems catching it … "

Her eyes focused on him again. "I'm sorry, Henry. I missed that … "

"I said: 'Who are you looking for'?"

She smiled awkwardly. "I am sorry. Was it that obvious?"

He did not know what she was talking about, so he kept quiet, hoping she would elaborate.

"I was supposed to meet someone; he's late."

"Who?"

"My contact in their organization. He telephoned to say he had something of importance to tell me … "

He was vastly relieved that there was a reason for her preoccupation. "So it's a working lunch?"

She relaxed at his mildness. "You did say you wanted to help!"

"I meant it – but I expect to be taken into your confidence first. It seems a bit of a one-sided arrangement."

"I would have told you – if it was necessary."

"What does that mean – *if* it was necessary?"

She glanced at her watch. "I can't be sure how far he can be trusted. As I said, he should have been here by now – although he did say I should be prepared to wait." She looked at him anxiously as though seeking his approval. "It sounds vague, I know. His last tip-off was good value, but this time the location was his suggestion. I agreed because it was a public place, which means it should be relatively safe, although that is why I chose this table – with our backs to the wall. When … *if* he comes I shall go over to join him, and you can watch my back."

I'd rather watch your front, Henry thought. He was pleased that she seemed to have faith in his ability to protect her. In fact, it was so gratifying that the reality of the situation held no fears for him. He felt confident enough to tackle Hassan himself if the giant should suddenly reappear.

At last their meal arrived in one large earthenware bowl. "Cous-cous," announced the proprietor with a flourish. He was followed by a young boy who produced two shallow dishes of water which Henry assumed were meant to be finger-bowls. He looked dubiously at the steaming bowl of food – a rich combination of meat or game, vegetables, dried fruits, and a type of semolina meal. With the bowl came spoons for the fine semolina, and Ruti advised him to play safe by using one. "The Muslims use their hands," she remarked. "Watch!"

She scooped her fingers into the hot grain and tossed it up

and down in the palm of her hand so that it formed a little dumpling; then with a deft movement of her thumb she popped it into her mouth. Henry looked on admiringly, but after the demonstration she picked up the other spoon. Her confidence was infectious, and although it looked a little greasy for Henry's taste, he realized he was hungry and decided to give it a whirl. They used their fingers to tackle the legs of chicken and chewed in silence until Henry used his other hand to move a chicken bone.

"Don't let anyone see you," she reprimanded. "They consider it unclean to use the left hand." At his startled look, she laughed and concluded: "I am only trying to educate you, Henry. As far as I am concerned you can eat with your feet!"

Henry shrugged morosely. "I'm sure it couldn't be any more difficult."

"Too rich for your palate?" she guessed.

"A little," he conceded. He rinsed his fingers and took a peach from the bowl of fresh fruit placed on the table, waving away the offer of mint tea. His stomach was ready to rebel.

Sensing his apprehension Ruti said: "You don't seem very sure of yourself. Would you be surprised to learn that cous-cous is regarded as a mild aphrodisiac?"

He smiled wryly. "I'm afraid it was wasted on me."

She took a packet of Gauloises from a small handbag and asked if he would mind her smoking. Lighting a cigarette she began to talk, relaxed again; no-one had come into the restaurant and she was able to concentrate her attention on Henry.

He asked her views on Israeli politics, but was not surprised when she refused to treat the question seriously. "I'm too busy staying alive to worry about politicians," she said.

"But aren't you answerable to them?"

"Are you?" Remembering that he had described himself as free-lance, she did not pursue the point. "People like us carry on regardless of who is in power and what their policies are."

"Carry on? Regardless of whether or not there is anything that needs to be done?"

She smiled. "When a country is surrounded by enemies there is always *too* much to do. In your country perhaps certain people have too little on their hands so they turn it into something of a game – but everything *we* do is for real."

"I don't know that there is much difference – the people in this business are much the same. All devious, and too clever by half."

"By half?"

He shrugged helplessly. "*Too* clever. The planners ... the faceless men behind the desks, not agents in the field ... " He was mentally comparing men like Beckton with Hamilton – and Ruti.

She laughed delightedly. " 'Too clever by half'! I've got it! That's just the trouble with the Jews ... Everyone thinks he knows best. When the nation's survival was threatened, you saw the best of us. Now we have more time to argue. Thank God the Arabs are no better."

Henry sniggered. "Funny thing – cleverness. I haven't met many of these nationalists, but I guess that Omar Rashid is as intelligent as most. Yet even he seems naîve. It's true that the Arabs form a natural entity, and that Islam could be a powerful unifying force, but it has always been a pipedream. They remember how near they came to it, but forget that history is littered with near misses. More to the point they even ignore the great Arab scholars. Take Ibn Khaldun, for example. Khaldun was pouring cold water on their ideas six hundred years ago. His reasons, if I remember correctly, are basically that everyone wants to rule the roost. Nothing has changed. The Syrians and Iraqis are still at each other's throats, as are the Libyans and Egyptians ... "

"But that is why we are here – not in those countries. Rashid's followers believe this is where the explosion will take place, and we think he could be right. People forget that Arab influence in this country goes back twelve hundred years."

Henry was beginning to find it difficult to concentrate on the discussion because he knew that an ominous rumbling in his intestines was advance warning of an impending conflagration between the cous-cous and his gastric juices. His mouth kept filling with fluid as though his tongue was sweating with anxiety, and his stomach was threatening to throw-up at the prospect of much more of that. Deciding it was expedient to excuse himself without delay, he headed for the toilet, grimly aware there was worse to come before it could get better. He made it just in time.

Although the ordeal was as bad as he had feared, the sickness soon passed over, and cold water splashed on his face and neck revived him enough to face the world again. A glance at his wristwatch indicated that nearly ten minutes had elapsed, and he was reluctant to leave the Israeli girl on her own any longer. It seemed unlikely that her contact was coming – perhaps, like Akhtar, he had been caught – but he wanted to get back.

During his short absence the café had begun to fill up. His gaze instinctively went to Ruti, apparently lost in thought until she was disturbed by the arrival of a small group of pedlars who had wandered in, seeking business. They were led by a shabbily-dressed youth selling newspapers and magazines; a boy who could have been his young brother had a tray of sweets, chocolates and a varied assortment of American chewing gum and cigarettes; another, older man, had his shoulders and arms weighed down by colourful carpets and rugs which, he announced to all and sundry, had been made locally. Finally, trailing several yards behind came a man selling oranges and grapefruit.

Henry watched mildly amused to see how the girl would cope as they came in turn to her table to try their individual brands of sales talk. She must have liked the youngest boy – scarcely more than a child – because she bought a few packs of chewing gum, but the others were waved away impatiently. Henry idly wondered what sort of money they could hope to earn in a café of this class. The carpet-seller, especially, might have been better employed tackling tourists at good class hotels such as the Balimar where there were a large number of guests with more money than sense. The proprietor too seemed to find their invasion undesirable – at least, from the business point of view – and he waved them away.

He was a tough-looking man, as Henry had already noticed, and whether it was his appearance that frightened them off, or whether it finally dawned on them that they had chosen the wrong establishment, three of the pedlars disappeared as though by the wave of a magic wand. It seemed to Henry that one minute they were there, and the next they were gone. However, the fruit-seller – presumably, because of his age, more experienced – took his time, and almost defiantly stopped at Ruti's table. Despite her insistence that she did not want to buy, he lifted the heavy tray from his shoulder, and rested it on the table top.

Henry had not completely recovered from his stomach upset and was feeling a little light-headed, but instinct warned him that the girl was in danger. The fruit-seller might just have been bloody-minded, but why pick on a girl sitting alone, when in a more crowded part of the café there were several groups who could have been more receptive?

Logic told him there might have been a number of reasons, but for once in his life he acted on impulse. He covered the dozen or so metres between himself and the girl's table at a gallop, and cannoned into the man, knocking him to the ground. He was conscious of Ruti's indrawn breath, and hoped his action was justified and he did not look too much of a fool.

Keeping his own balance, he snatched at the tray of fruit and hurled it as hard as he could in the direction of one of the open entrances. Considering its ponderous bulk it was a good shot, but the tray caught the edge of the door frame breaking its momentum, and some of the citrus fruit was dislodged and bounced back into the café, while the rest landed on the pavement outside. Henry watched, fascinated, as the rather inferior oranges and grapefruit traced separate paths. No-one moved – no-one had time to move – before the explosion which wrecked that end of the café.

Horrified, Henry momentarily forgot Ruti and the would-be assassin, and as the choking dust began to clear he rushed to get to those who had been injured. At least three had been trapped by debris – large slabs of plaster from the ceiling and sand-stone from the walls had collapsed – and with other customers he used his hands to free them. The proprietor stood by helplessly, stunned by the disaster that had suddenly overtaken his source of livelihood.

Apart from one man who had been killed by a bulky light-fitting, the other injuries were only superficial. Realizing there was little more he could do, Henry stood back and looked for Ruti. She was grim-faced, shocked by the devastation but angry that she had been distracted enough to allow the fruit-seller to escape. He squeezed her shoulder reassuringly.

But she had recovered her composure. "There's nothing we can do here," she pointed out. "We had better leave before the police come."

Henry nodded. "I have a hunch that one of Inspector Khan's men followed us, and I don't fancy having to explain this." He was satisfied with the way he had acted, and rather pleased that she had not made a fuss about saving her life – as though she accepted him as an equal, taking his skills for granted.

There was chaos in the café; people in varying stages of excitement and hysteria, concerned for the injured or heatedly debating wild theories, so he and the girl simply walked out. Two minutes later the police arrived in force, and threw a cordon around the building.

Seven

On their return to the Balimar, Henry was determined not to take 'no' for an answer in asking when they might meet again, but in the event it was the girl who took the initiative. It was perhaps the way she touched the back of his hand that made him sense her manner had changed. She studied him very seriously before leaning over to kiss him lightly on the lips, and adding a simple "thank you". The kiss was a gesture of friendship more than anything else, but he knew that it established a platform upon which to develop the relationship and his spirits soared.

It flashed through his mind that the change in her attitude might have been a cue for him to be bolder, as James Bond or John Hamilton might have been, but he held back – not because he was apprehensive, but because even in his new-found confidence he thought of her as someone special.

"I will tell my people what happened," she said, "I hope it will make a difference."

"You mean they might allow us to meet openly? Am I supposed to be grateful for small mercies?"

"Are your people any different?" she asked.

He shrugged. "Presumably this means that I'm still not even eligible for your telephone number?"

She smiled and squeezed his hand. "I will telephone *you* – I promise."

On entering the hotel his thoughts were confused. He acknowledged the fact that the Israeli girl was a trained agent well able to look after herself, but he felt strangely protective towards her. Commonsense told him he should be on the first flight to London, but the experience in the café made him feel a new man. Luck had been with him, admittedly, but no-one could deny that he had responded to the challenge in a way that would not have discredited someone of Hamilton's calibre. Luck, after all, could be even more important than ability, as he should have realized when Hamilton's ran out.

His indecision was not helped by a sense of outrage at what Rashid believed was justified for the sake of the Cause. He recalled passionate arguments in his student days with his flatmate, Doug Fenton, an armchair revolutionary, whose defence of terrorism had been encapsulated in the same argument always: "It all depends on the Cause."

Henry decided that someone else must make the decision for him. It was late afternoon and, with any luck, Beckton might still be available. He had no idea where Beckton's office was, but he had been given a telephone number that Heather might use. *Heather*! He suddenly realized that his fiancée had entered his thoughts only once – and then only when he had been feeling sorry for himself. Now he was day-dreaming like a love-sick schoolboy about an Israeli girl he had known a couple of days, as though there were no commitments and he was free to play the field. He managed to contain his conscience after something of a struggle; the circumstances were exceptional, after all. He remembered his parents talking about the war and the people had lived for the day in the knowledge that there might not be a tomorrow. Surely it was the same for him? Within a matter of days, he might have been killed on at least three occasions.

He put in a call to the London number in his possession, telling the man who answered to get Beckton to phone him back. From the pained voice at the other end, Henry sensed that he was committing a huge indiscretion using real names on an open line, but he was beyond caring. He needed someone in authority to put an end to his quandary, and his principal fear was that Beckton would simply forget him. He was marginally surprised fifteen minutes later when Beckton returned his call, sounding like a long-lost uncle.

"My dear boy," he began as though Henry's reappearance had been the highlight of his day. "How have you been?"

Henry was not impressed. Beckton ought to have made contact as soon as he heard of Hamilton's death. However, he conceded that Beckton probably had a wide range of responsibilities and possibly good reason for remaining in the background, so he kept his irritation under rein. "I don't know how much I can say on the phone," he speculated.

"This line is OK – feel free … "

"You know what happened to Hamilton?"

"Mmm. Poor devil."

"And to me?"

"If you mean since then, the answer is no. *Nothing*, I hope."

"I was kidnapped by the man who shot Hamilton."

Beckton must have been surprised because it took several seconds for him to react. "Kidnapped?" He paused as though giving Henry an opportunity to correct him. " … And by the people who killed … Is this something they admitted?"

"And a lot more. If I hadn't escaped, I wouldn't have been speaking to you now, or ever."

"Good Lord! I had no idea you were even at risk. I

promise you we wanted someone to identify a few manuscripts. Heaven knows what went wrong ... "

"I should have thought that was obvious. They *knew* about Hamilton – someone betrayed you!"

"Look, let's deal with you first, Mr Franklin ... Henry. I don't want any more to happen to you. What flight are you catching?"

"That's why I wanted to speak to you. When I escaped I couldn't wait to get out of the country, but now I'm having second thoughts. I'd like to get my own back on those bastards."

"Your own back?"

"A couple of hours ago they blew up a restaurant on the outskirts of Karachi. Guess who survived by the skin of his teeth?"

"Good Lord!" Beckton paused to reflect: "That's the second time I've said that! I *never* say 'Good Lord'! On the other hand I'm not in the habit of having this kind of conversation with people outside the department. What is going on? Why should they be after you? Assuming the explosion *was* intended for you?"

Henry decided it was simpler not to mention Ruti. "The point is: what is the best course of action for me? By getting even with these people I must be helping you. I don't know what John Hamilton's mission was – apart from getting the manuscripts back – and I'm not kidding myself I can step into his shoes, but I must be better than no-one, and I'm quite friendly with one of the local police inspectors ... "

" ... Wait a minute, Mr Franklin – Henry!" Beckton interjected. "Your attitude is highly commendable, and I thank you for wanting to help, but I don't think we can accept the responsibility."

"*What* responsibility? And isn't it a bit late for that anyway?"

"I admit to a miscalculation on my part. But since you've managed to survive our inefficiency, it's obviously not too late to make amends."

"But I'm *volunteering*!"

"The responsibility is to others ... your family ... to your fiancée. The office took a call from her the other day. Seems she was worried you hadn't been in touch. They told her you had gone to Paris on a special assignment – and she seemed to accept that ... assumed it was some recognition of your talents ... Sounds like a fine young woman."

"Well, if you order me to come back ... ?" Henry began.

"Mr Franklin ... Henry, I cannot *order* you to do anything – any more than I ordered you to go to Karachi. But speaking as a friend, I think you would be well advised to come back as soon as possible."

"Don't you care about Hamilton?"

"Come now, dear boy, there's no need to be offensive," Beckton replied. "John and I were very close; he was like a son. His replacement happens to be one of his friends, so you need not worry on that score."

"That's all very well, but I already know more about these people than your man can pick up in a month of Sundays. I *know* them. They actually took me on an assignment – to poison the city's water supply – that's the sort of people they are ... " He stopped to allow Beckton to comment, but the voice at the other end was silent. "The only way I could prevent a catastrophe, was ... " He hesitated before concluding: " ... The only way I could *stop* them was to kill the guy in charge."

"Kill? You *killed* someone!"

"It was him or me. Don't worry, Mr Beckton, no-one knows I was involved."

"Except their people."

"Presumably."

Beckton sighed. "I recruited a librarian for a routine assignment, and he's already killed someone ... " he said, as though thinking aloud.

Henry stifled a bitter laugh. "It's strange to hear someone refer to me as a librarian. Everyone else, including the police, thinks it's just a cover for my real job."

"I would be careful what you say to the police, Henry."

"I am."

"I take my hat off to you. I still think you should come back, but perhaps it would not be a bad idea to wait a day or so until Hamilton's replacement turns up. At least you can give him a proper briefing."

"What's his name?"

"Oh, he'll make himself known to you. In the circumstances, the less said the better. Meanwhile, don't do anything foolhardy."

"You must be joking! I spoke about getting even with this chap Rashid, but I was thinking about gathering evidence – so that someone else can deal with him. Inspector Khan says ... "

"Leave the police out of it, Henry," Beckton urged. "Apart from anything else, you don't know who might be working for Rashid. If you need advice or assistance, go to Crawford at the embassy."

"I don't trust that man."

"You have my assurance ... "

"You don't have to believe *me*. John Hamilton didn't trust him. Now I'm convinced he's working with Rashid."

"Henry, if you want help, I'm going to have to pull rank. All I can say is that in this business things are not always what they seem to be. I can't spell it out."

The penny dropped as it dawned on Henry that Crawford had probably managed to infiltrate Rashid's organization; somehow managed to gain his confidence. Inevitably he would have to provide certain scraps of information to maintain his credibility. "All right," he conceded. "I'll wait for your man to turn up. Meanwhile, I would be grateful if someone could telephone my fiancée. Just to keep her happy."

Replacing the receiver, Henry realized that if he hoped to make a positive contribution time was not on his side. The only person to whom he could turn – assuming that Beckton knew what he was talking about – was Crawford. He picked up the phone again.

The colonel sounded irritable. "What happened to you?" he demanded. "I told you to wait until your passport had been returned!"

Henry decided not to make an issue of his suspicions. "It's a long story. Look, I'm phoning on Beckton's instructions. He thinks it's time we were more aggressive ... take the initiative rather than wait for them to act. What do you know about Omar Rashid?"

"How do *you* know about Rashid?"

Henry laughed. "Would *you* answer a question like that? Let's just say I know a little; I want to know a lot more ... "

"Wouldn't we all? Anyway, what I know is privileged information."

"Then phone Beckton if you must, but I need to know quickly."

"What is the panic?"

"That's something you take up with Beckton too, if you're prepared to waste *his* time ... "

Crawford hesitated before replying. "You say you've just spoken to him?"

"A couple of minutes ago."

"Very well. I suppose if London chooses to treat me as a post-box, there's little I can do about it. I told them about Rashid *months* ago ... "

"*What* did you tell them?"

"Well … there wasn't very much to tell … I just warned them," he blustered. "You probably know he keeps a low profile. I've taken a special interest in the man but I still know next to nothing. Tell me what *you* know, and I'll try to fill in the gaps … "

Henry hesitated, doubtful about the wisdom of revealing too much. "All I really know is that he runs a small but well-organized revolutionary group. To the world at large he is ostensibly a newspaper editor. That's his cover, but what about the man beneath?"

"Aha!" said Crawford with what seemed like a note of triumph. "That is what we would all like to know. It is difficult to draw a distinction between the public face and the real person. All I can say is that he is well respected in political circles."

"Where does he get his funding?"

"No idea. I believe he actually owns the paper, but that must barely break even."

"How vulnerable is he?"

"To his enemies? We did a little digging, but didn't come up with anything. No weaknesses as far as we could ascertain."

"*No* vices?"

"None that we are aware of. Not that he is a religious man, as he sometimes pretends – to impress the more devout followers. He has been seen with women, and to gamble a little, but everything in moderation."

"Where would he do these things?"

"Gamble? There are only a couple of respectable casinos – at least, in the sense that they are licensed – still permitted to operate by the authorities. I think he goes to a place called the *Cage D'Or* … "

There was a hubbub in the hotel reception area, and as he approached, Henry sensed the tension. The buzz of voices was angry, as though people were not talking but arguing, some in whispers but others shouting and gesticulating. The topic could only have been news of dramatic proportions. Wondering if it had anything to do with the explosion, he caught the eye of the assistant manager who responded with a gesture to go over. The solemn expression indicated that the news they had received was depressing. As Henry squeezed through the congested foyer the atmosphere seemed potentially explosive.

"Terrible news, Mr Franklin," the assistant manager confirmed. "Our President has been assassinated."

Henry was stunned. "*The* president? Ahmed Byoussi?"

The Pakistani nodded.

"But who would want to kill Doctor Boussi? Surely he had no enemies?"

"The world has gone mad," the man responded with a shrug. "He was the most popular leader since Jinnah. They say India is responsible ... "

"*They* say?"

"Rumour has it. India or Bangladesh."

"Do you believe that?"

"Who knows what to believe? What other enemies do we have apart from the CIA and the Zionists?"

"That sounds even more far-fetched. What happened?"

"His car was blown up outside Government House."

"When was this?"

"This morning."

Henry felt a load lift from his shoulders. Remembering the plot to poison the water supply, he had little doubt that the people blamed by the rumour mongers were probably the last to be involved, but it was reassuring nevertheless to know that Ruti had not even been in the same city. As he walked away he wondered about the coincidence of a second bomb intended for the girl. It sounded like Rashid's style – to imply that the assassin had later been blown up by one of her own bombs ... He toyed with the idea of phoning Khan with the theory, but decided that the Inspector probably had enough on his plate without wild speculation.

Meanwhile he did not have time to waste in theorizing if Rashid's background was to be investigated.

The *Cage D'Or* casino was a large, white, modern building set in several acres of private woodland. The whole of the surrounding area was kept in perpetual eerie darkness except for an intermittent red glow from a flashing neon name sign across the flat roof. The club was advertised in most of the official guides to Karachi with the location clearly marked, together with the route from the main road indicated by red arrows. Henry hired a small car but once the club was within walking distance he left the car parked by a huge hoarding on the main highway, going the rest of the way on foot. After a while he left the road altogether and approached his destination under the cover of the trees. In fact, the stealth seemed to be unnecessary because, apart from a couple of unoccupied cars, the courtyard and terrace in front of the club were deserted; nor were there apparently any lights on inside the building.

Trying to imagine what Hamilton would have done in the circumstances, he avoided the front entrance and skirted the house, following a narrow sand and gravel footpath to the back. Here the scene presented a remarkable contrast; there were between forty and fifty cars parked in an orderly fashion, having apparently entered the grounds from another road at the back which was not marked on his map, and which was not apparently intended for the tourist trade. Satisfied that this was most probably the entrance used by "members" or private parties, he returned to the front of the building, and rang the bell.

He had to ring a second time before there was any response, and eventually the heavy wooden door was opened a crack by a woman whose face was indistinguishable in the gloom. When she said nothing he enquired about the casino, asking if it was open. Like a wide-eyed tourist who might assume she did not understand English, he emphasized his meaning by indicating the flashing sign.

Giving no clue that she knew what he was talking about – or cared – the woman nevertheless opened the door a fraction wider and gestured him to follow her. She led the way through a darkened corridor into a large circular room which he assumed was a nightclub. With bad grace she pointed to the bar as though to say: if you *must* come to the club, at least let us see the colour of your money.

Despite the surly introduction, the atmosphere was quite welcoming; the decor bright, modern, and – if somewhat unrestrained – at least in good taste. There was a tiny dance floor in the centre, a kaleidoscope of coloured tiles lit from below and offset by the black sheen of the rest of the floor. The curved bar running almost half the circumference was decorated in sumptuous red leather and velvet and backed by sweeping mirrors so that customers sitting at the bar could see what was going on behind them. At the far end of the room, only partially concealed by expensive-looking heavy curtains, was the casino.

Had he not already seen the cars tucked away at the back, Henry would have wondered why the club seemed so empty. The room was big enough to seat a couple of hundred people in relative comfort, yet there were not more than twenty, apart from him – and dotted about as they were, made the place seem even emptier. Without making a closer inspection, he thought he could make out a handful of gamblers in the casino part of the club. Where on earth were the owners of the cars out back?

A sliding hatch behind the cash desk at the bar provided the first clue when he became aware of trays of drinks being loaded on a dumb waiter, interspersed with cheques or bank notes in payment of mysterious bills. As he sipped what he knew to be heavily diluted Scotch whisky, he planned his strategy. He was taking a chance on Rashid putting in an appearance and, in any case, he could hardly march up to him like an old friend. The ideal situation was to observe without being spotted, but that was difficult while there were so few people about. He wondered about the destination of the drinks on the dumb waiter, and how one earned the 'privilege' of being invited into what was presumably a more select part of the club.

However, the thought was pushed to one side by the sudden appearance on the stool next to him of a pretty red-haired European woman in a very low-cut cocktail dress. Although she could only be one of the club's hostesses, the girl – in her middle twenties – had an engaging freshness that seemed out of character, and intrigued him. He was not familiar with the scene but even her introductory patter was disarmingly different to what he expected, and he could not object to buying her one of the imitation whiskies. Her English left much to be desired, but if the grammar was bad the vocabulary was quite wide and there was an infectious enthusiasm about her conversation that enabled him to get the sense of even the most confused sentence.

Having assumed the *Cage D'Or* was a conventional casino, he had not contemplated the prospect of female company, but he had time to kill, and the girl – she told him her name was Helga, and that she was German – was good company.

Although lacking Ruti's character, she made a fair stand-in for an evening out. She told him in her guttural English that she had been an airline stewardess, but liked Pakistan because of the climate, and – she added with a roguish smile – for the money she was able to earn. They were in the middle of a mildly entertaining conversation about Hamburg, when without warning she leaned over and whispered in his ear: "You would like make loving?"

The suddenness of the proposal took the wind from his sails for a moment. " ... Now?" he responded tamely.

"Yes, why not?"

"Where?"

"Upstairs ... "

For a few moments the thought of going to bed with Helga for a few pounds was tempting. His sex-life during the few past weeks had been somewhat neglected, and the idea of paying for the experience seemed less compromising. However, his conscience – reminding him how little time he had – spoiled the prospect, and he politely declined. "I'm convalescing," he lied. "Malaria. I'm still weak ... "

Keeping her voice at a whisper, she said: "Please come. We can talk there." Having already turned down the invitation, he wondered what there was to talk about, and sensing the resistance, she added, her face an unfamiliarly serious mask: "You give me English money or dollars: I will give you much information. You want it?"

He did not have to ask her what she meant – there could be only one explanation, but he was immediately suspicious. "How did you know I'm buying?" he asked.

Helga looked anxiously at the woman behind the cash register. She returned the girl's look blandly, but Henry realized she was keeping a close eye on the activities of all her girls. With the faintest inclination of her head in that direction, Helga whispered: "Madam is telling me. I will explain. Please go now!"

Henry had no idea whether he could trust her, but the apparent frankness impressed him and he decided to take a chance. He followed her out of the room, up a flight of stairs and along another corridor – this one dimly lit – to her room.

As she fumbled in her tiny purse for the key, it occurred to him that "Madam" had been remarkably well informed. As far as he could judge, only one person might have known his intention to go to the *Cage D'Or* that night, and that one person had yet to prove he could be trusted.

Helga's room matched her personality. Bright and gay, it impressed on first sight but after the surface glamour had been scratched, there was nothing else of note. Dominating the rest of the room was a large bed; as though because that was the source of her income, it had to be the focal point.

He followed her in warily, half expecting to find someone concealed behind the door, but because Helga seemed so genuinely intent on some scheme of her own, his assurance quickly returned. There was another door at one end and he opened it to ensure that no-one was hiding in there, but it turned out to be the lavatory.

When he was satisfied, Helga asked for the customary 100 rupees "house fee" to allay Madam's suspicions, explaining that her normal fee was anything a man cared to give in excess of that figure. Henry had no intention of parting with any money at all until she had explained her mysterious behaviour – yet again he found her willing to come straight to the point.

"When you are arriving tonight, Madam tells me you were English policeman. She say I must take you to the room, to ask many questions – men always telling me what I wish to know," she confessed without a hint of false modesty.

He asked her why she had disobeyed those orders.

"Because I have the head – or as you British say the 'nose' – for money," she admitted with a disarming smile. "I think if you have information valuable to Madam and her friends, then you will be interested in them – interested enough to pay Helga a reward … !"

He hedged. "I might be … depends on what I thought it was worth."

But Helga was master of the situation; she had everything worked out and her confidence was reflected in her words: "For one hundred English pounds I can be telling the name of the man who answers all your question. If you do not have the monies with your body, I will trust to getting it tomorrow."

"Why should you wish to help me?" he enquired cautiously. "If you know this man, you must appreciate the danger involved. If his friends find out that you were my informant, they could kill you – and not very pleasantly … "

"I am knowing the risk," she said, her pretty face strangely solemn, "but I go to Germany in the three weeks, or sooner if can be, so I am not worrying. In any case, unless *you* tell him, what reason for him to know it is me?"

Henry raised his eyebrows. "And you would do this … risk your life … for one hundred pounds?"

She laughed. "If you knowing me better, you must understand there is very small things I will not do for the money! I ask one hundred pounds because I am not greedy being; I think it is the correct value. I am saving to my future, and everything is counting. As well as the generous gifts I am having from my rich customers, it will help my savings for my own broth … no, I am meaning 'establishment'." She struggled with the last word, but he was left in no doubt as to the purpose of the place.

Henry shrugged. "All right I'll see that you get the money, provided I think the information is worth it."

Helga smiled demurely, and he could not help thinking what a delightful, scheming little vixen she was. "Good," she commented. "I am liking you. Why not you taking off your jacket." She walked over slowly, put her arms round his neck, and added: "No charging to my friends ... "

He felt hot under the collar and a stirring in his pants, but controlled the natural impulse. "Business before pleasure," he said with a regretful smile to show that he was normal.

She merely tightened her arms about him and snuggled up closer, but gently he disengaged her grip. "Well? Who is this person?" he demanded.

Helga looked hurt at the rebuff, but she was too good a business-woman to allow pride to interfere. "His name is Omar Rashid."

Henry was momentarily confused. He did not know whether he was disappointed at hearing something he thought he already knew, or whether he should be grateful for confirmation from an independent source. "I already know the name," he said guardedly, "but what can you tell me about him?"

"He is a bad man."

He controlled his exasperation. "You'll have to do better than that!"

"He come here."

"You mean to you?"

She shook her head. "He come to club all the time ... "

"So what? He is known to be a gambler."

"Not just to casino. Sometimes up the stairs ... here. The girls are thinking he has much money for throwing in the fire, but I think he put money back to own pockets. I am thinking he is owning this house."

The theory sounded attractive to Henry; the *Cage D'Or* would provide a considerable revenue. However, for the moment it remained an idle speculation and he asked why she suspected he might be her real employer.

Helga lay down on the bed and lit a cigarette from a pack in her bag. He refused one himself and sat down almost gingerly on the edge of the bed, doubting whether his self-control would stand the test if he moved any closer.

"He has the influence over Madam; she has fear of him. He is having a bodyguard called Hassan. This man is one of my customers, and is not paying the house-fee ... "

Henry found it difficult not to react at the mention of Hassan, but he realized there was no reason why Helga should know he was dead.

Unaware of his thoughts she continued: "A servant is not coming to a broth ... establishment like this. It is not cheap. Many customers are from Europe, others are rich merchants, or those who have ... how you say: expense accounts?"

The fact that the late, unlamented Hassan's visits might have been subsidized by the club itself, had a ring of truth. "What sort of man is this Hassan?" he asked.

She wrinkled her brow with concentration. "It is difficult. He is kind of man my mother warn her children: do not be naughty – or bogeymen will come. The girls here are also frightened. Yet for me he is gentle as puppy. At first I close my eyes when he make love, but now I am finding him interesting – like wild animal."

Henry ignored the mental picture her words conjured-up, and asked: "Does he talk much – about what he does, I mean?"

"Of course. We are like confessor ... no, like priest. Men are wishing to talk, to unburden their soul. At first I am curious, and I flatter him – I am telling him how important he is looking. Now he trusts me and he is talking; I no have to ask. There is nothing secret, I am thinking; only the gossip. It is good for him I not police informer ... "

Henry laughed. "What about me then? Or don't you regard me as a policeman?"

"You are from different country," she replied quite seriously, as though the difference was obvious. "Also, you are more curious of his master, so I do not betray Hassan ... "

He shook his head reassuringly. "What sort of things does he tell you about Rashid?"

The girl thought for a moment and admitted: "I am not knowing what is of interest for you, but he is saying that Rashid will be president of Pakistan one day soon ... "

"You mean now that Doctor Byoussi is dead?"

She shrugged. "I am not understanding the politics. He say Rashid clever man. He have secret papers to explode the Government when he publish them ... "

"*Explode?* Blow up? Overthrow?"

"Overthrow government," she confirmed. "He keep them locked up until the fruit ... the *time* is ripe ... "

Henry sighed. "The sixty-four dollar question ... !"

She stopped, puzzled by the expression, and he added: "I don't suppose he gave any clue as to when that might be?"

She shrugged.

"Think ... it might be important," he urged.

She seemed to make an effort, but her expression implied that it was all a waste of time. "He says nothing, and I am thinking he does not know. Why must Rashid tell his servant when he will publish?" Henry was prepared to concede defeat, but suddenly she remembered something. "They will take the papers with them to Cairo ... "

"Where?"

"Cairo. I am not understanding also, but Hassan is saying they will go this weekend, on the Holy Day ... Friday."

"Forget Rashid's own newspaper. Why are they going to Egypt: did he tell you?"

"It is no secret. There is meeting ... *conference* of Muslim newspaper editors. That is the reason."

Henry decided on the spot he had to get these documents to Inspector Khan before Rashid had an opportunity of getting them out of the country. Even as the idea struck him he was impatient to get on with it. "I think I'll find some excuse for going along to see Mr Rashid – tomorrow, or the next day," he lied. "Do you know the address by any chance?"

"Yes, the office is living in South Napier Street. I am not knowing the number but you will recognize the building, or you can telephone first."

To avoid arousing her suspicion he delayed his departure by asking a few more innocuous questions about Hassan, listening impatiently to her replies. After five minutes he looked at his watch, saw that it was two minutes to midnight, and announced that he would have to leave because he had to be up early in the morning. "I'm supposed to be convalescing," he explained.

Showing him to the door, she asked when she would get her money.

"Tomorrow or the next day," he replied as truthfully as he could, hoping that Colonel Crawford had some sort of contingency fund. "I'll bring it myself," he promised, "and then perhaps we can forget business."

Helga studied him somewhat coyly: "The malaria will be finished?"

With the aid of the street guide that came with the car, he found the newspaper building quite easily. He drove past slowly, and turned into a side street 100 yards further along. Then he made a casual reconnaissance of the area, strolling round the block to get a rough idea of the layout.

Despite the late hour he put in a call to Khan, but as he

had feared the inspector was off-duty, and he could not think of an appropriate message. Anything that spelt out the importance of his discovery might find its way to Rashid through one of his many informers – anything else was pointless if it meant waiting until Khan returned to duty; by the time a search warrant was obtained, the incriminating papers might have been removed. The logical course of action was to try at least to break-in and get them himself.

Although he had never even contemplated burglary, let alone actually carry it out, it seemed that the odds on getting into a newspaper office – as opposed to a high security building – were hardly insurmountable; in any case, if it was beyond him he could always fall back on the police later. Meanwhile, he crossed his fingers that caution and commonsense might compensate for his lack of experience.

Although there was not a soul about instinct warned him to avoid the front of the building which was overlooked, and he discovered that the back entrance was separated from the road only by a small walled courtyard. Being tall, he was able to scale the wall without difficulty, hurrying across the open courtyard – expecting any moment to see a light go on in one of the adjoining properties. He found the door was locked, and rather than force it and risk making a noise in the stillness, he looked at the nearest windows. The first one he tried was unlocked – something he had half expected; there was little in a newspaper office to attract thieves in normal circumstances, and a member of the office staff might have left this and other windows open slightly to air the place.

With bated breath he climbed through into an outer office. Doing everything by what he imagined to be the 'book', and having no gloves with him, he wiped the window frame and sill with his handkerchief before going any further. He knew he was being over-cautious since his fingerprints would mean nothing to the local police, but he was not prepared to take any chances. He gave the room only a cursory glance – he was looking for Rashid's private office, and he discovered it through a name plate conveniently fixed to the door. It was unlocked – for the benefit of the cleaners, he guessed from the number of empty metal waste bins left on top of desks in the outer office. Entering the room his attention was immediately riveted to a large safe behind Rashid's desk.

Henry tried to imagine himself in Hamilton's shoes. To his untutored eye the safe did not seem particularly modern, but it was formidable enough to unnerve him. For a moment he was tempted to give up on the spot, but on closer inspection he realized his luck was still holding – the safe was operated by what looked like a conventional combination system. The principle had been explained and demonstrated at a conference on security he had attended with fellow librarians six months before. He had given less than his full attention at the time, but inevitably some of the lecture had rubbed off, which meant that with a little patience, ingenuity – and luck – there was a faint chance it might just be crackable.

There were large windows on either side of the safe; both had venetian blinds and for a fleeting moment he was tempted to pull them down to ensure his privacy, but he decided to work by the light of the moon. Reasonably confident that there was no nightwatchman to disturb him, Henry was able to give his mind entirely to the task ahead. First he examined the surrounding area in the faint hope that Rashid had scratched the number on the steel surface, but it was a forlorn hope and then he had to start work in earnest.

Before long his knees were aching and he had to change his position every few minutes. The combination of humidity and his intense concentration made him begin to sweat; the scattered globules quickly became a torrent. As he worked on he became edgy, beginning to wonder if he was not wasting his time. Suppose the safe was stuffed with office files, and that more valuable papers were tucked away in some sophisticated wall safe? But despite such anxieties, he persisted in the knowledge that he had all night if necessary.

In the circumstances time dragged, but at the back of his mind the memory of what the expert at the conference had told him and his colleagues — that the series of numbers selected often conformed to a limited group of variations on a set formula, and this was influenced by the owner's way of thinking; it could be 'merely' a question of running through the possible permutations until he found the right one. He only hoped that Rashid, just to be awkward, had not worked in Urdu.

Then, tantalizingly it swung open with a gentle click — as though until now it had been merely testing him. He strained his eyes to peer inside. The safe was empty except for a sheaf of papers on the middle shelf, gleaming as the light penetrated the inner blackness. With a hand that trembled slightly from the nervous exertion of the past thirty minutes, he reached inside and drew them out. In the gloom it was not easy to read small print, and as he held them closer a bead of perspiration dropped from his glistening forehead on to the papers and made them vibrate in the silence. The whiteness of the papers seemed to hypnotize him, and as he stared, his disquieting thoughts became the horrifying realization. The "documents" were just blank sheets of paper.

The implication was so painfully obvious that he was not terribly surprised when the room was suddenly flooded with light. Dazzled by the unaccustomed brightness, he could barely discern a couple of silhouettes standing just inside the door. Gradually the blurred forms materialized into the recognizable shapes of Rashid and another man he imagined to be one of the young guards. The younger man, his face impassive, held a gun pointed at his stomach, but Rashid, hand still poised at the light switch, was obviously delighted. "You didn't *really* believe I would leave valuables lying about like that, Mr Franklin?" he asked.

Still squatting helplessly on the floor, Henry realized how blindly he had walked – even hurried – into the baited trap. And as Rashid addressed his new bodyguard in Urdu he knew without any doubt at all that Helga had outsmarted him. Her talk of intimate conversations with Hassan had been a complete fabrication – he should have remembered Hassan spoke only Urdu.

Eight

Henry made no effort to get up; if nothing else he presented a smaller target with his long frame crouched behind the desk. Having been caught red-handed, he no longer had any feelings of apprehension, only frustrating anger at his gullibility. Yet someone in an adjoining office might have imagined it was an ordinary business meeting from the casual tone in which he responded: "What now, Mr Rashid?"

Rashid's raised eyebrows indicated surprise at the naïvety of his question. "*Now*, Mr Franklin?" He glanced at his watch. "In approximately three minutes time there will be no more 'now' for you – only an unlamented past."

"Three minutes?"

"When you will be shot like a common thief … "

"Not even a court martial?" Henry's knees were beginning to ache so he got up and cautiously stretched himself.

Rashid failed to get the significance of his reference to Akhtar. "We shall say there was no time to phone the police," he said. "We simply interrupted you breaking into my safe, and you were shot while trying to escape." He drew a fat wad of banknotes from his hip pocket and held them up. "This evidence of your guilt will be found clutched in your hand."

Henry's mind went blank. It was not as though he was scared, but he felt out of his depth. In desperation he sought inspiration from his hero, John Hamilton, and it seemed to work because almost immediately he felt the pressures ease. He was conscious of a sneer forming on his lips. "Isn't someone going to wonder what you were doing here at this hour in the morning? It's not as though it was even your day for going to press!"

Rashid shrugged lightly. "No mystery at all. Our evidence will be something like this: We were returning home from a casino just outside the city and had to pass this way. We saw a light on and thought for a moment that it was the fault of a cleaner, but then my young friend, whose eyes are sharper than mine, said he could make out a shadow moving about. We came to investigate and surprised you in front of the open safe. You managed to break away, and in the struggle the gun went off and – well, I'm afraid you were killed! Naturally we were appalled at such an unfortunate loss of life, but then we are not used to dealing with international criminals. You looked desperate enough for anything … "

Henry played for time. "I'd be more scared if I thought you really intended to kill me – but I'm satisfied you're too shrewd. Karachi has turned into such an unhealthy city for tourists, that even the police are embarrassed. Besides, my government already knows enough about you to begin applying pressure in certain circles – and when they do, how long do you think you can survive?"

Rashid looked at his watch again. "Your time has run out, Mr Franklin," he said reproachfully, "but as much of what you say makes sense, I will not shoot you here, after all. A little subtlety might be in order, so I think that we will chase you onto the roof and allow you to lose your footing in the dark." He gave a sharp Urdu command to his bodyguard who pocketed his gun with the intention of overpowering the Englishman. But that momentary slackening of his concentration was long enough for Henry to act.

Grabbing the sharp-edged metal bin from under the desk, he hurled it at the Pakistani, catching him squarely over the eyes. The man fell back partially dazed, and Henry leapt after him instinctively, retrieved the bin and cracked him solidly over the head with it. This time the young man collapsed heavily against a bookcase, causing it to overbalance, its contents emptying through the glass front – showering the inert form with glass splinters and a hundred or so heavy volumes.

Henry then turned to face Rashid. He may not have been a trained fighter, but in his new-found confidence it did not even occur to him that he could not overpower the smaller man. In any case, instinct told him that Rashid was an organizer who relied on others to handle the rough stuff. Even so, Henry did not rush his fences. Watching Rashid carefully, he reached down for the gun in the unconscious man's jacket pocket. Rashid was apparently unarmed and his eyes blinked nervously when he saw his henchman's gun in the Englishman's hand.

Henry had never held a gun in anger and although he had no intention of shooting anyone, the sense of power was uplifting. There was an impasse for several seconds, but finally Henry knew what to do. He leapt forward, the butt of the gun smashing into the side of Rashid's jaw. As the Pathan collapsed, Henry fled, escaping through the window from which he had entered. Suspecting that neither man would regain consciousness for several minutes, he took no chances nevertheless, and continued running until he had reached the car. Then he dropped the gun in the gutter and drove off.

Back in his room at the hotel, Henry's mind was too restless for sleep. Closing his eyes was a signal for the events of the past few hours to be re-enacted over and over again. Eventually, when their significance had been blunted by repetition, his thoughts returned to the more insidious problem of how Rashid had learned of his intention to visit the *Cage D'Or*.

The information could only have come from Crawford; the colonel was the only person who knew. Yet what was the purpose? If Beckton was right and Crawford was really working against Rashid, then the only explanation could be that he considered Henry to be handy bait, and expendable.

He woke in a sweat and looked at his watch on the bedside cabinet. It was 11.25 am, and with every single cell in his brain seeming individually to resist the idea of getting out of bed, he – or rather a numb, mindless body, managed to make it to the bathroom. Under an alternately invigorating and soothing shower, his brain began to stir, and by the time he had dried himself he was feeling almost alive. So, although he had walked past the spot to and from the bathroom, it was not until he moved over to the telephone to ask room service for a light breakfast to be sent up, that he noticed a white envelope that had been slipped under the front door of the suite. Curiously he picked it up, removed the note inside and read;

WE ARE TIRED OF YOUR INTERFERENCE. THIS MUST STOP *IMMEDIATELY*, OR YOU WILL NOT SEE YOUR FRIEND MISS KENAN ALIVE AGAIN. SHE WILL BE RELEASED ONLY WHEN WE ARE CERTAIN YOU ARE LEAVING THE COUNTRY.

"A FRIEND"

The wording may have been melodramatic, but its impact

was that of a sledgehammer, and the last cobwebs of sleep were washed away by the sweat that engulfed him. To say that he was unnerved would have been an understatement – he was almost frantic with concern, and even his recent trick of putting himself in John Hamilton's shoes failed to help – especially since he suspected that Hamilton would have been disciplined enough not to allow personal feelings to interfere with his judgement.

Whoever had written the note – and he could only assume it had been Rashid – was not bluffing, and although she had probably been identified as an Israeli agent, they must have seen Ruti and him together and found his Achilles heel.

There had been none of the usual warnings about going to the police; they had not considered it necessary. Their mistake was that Henry was not the Intelligence agent they took him to be: nor could they have appreciated his desperation, or the fact that the only person to whom he *could* turn was a policeman – Inspector Khan. Hamilton may not have approved, but Henry reminded himself that Hamilton was not infallible – and to prove it, he was dead. He picked up the phone.

"Why should they be so desperate to see the back of *you*, Mr Franklin?" Khan demanded over coffee in the hotel restaurant.

"I don't know," Henry protested. "I can only imagine they think I've got some information about them that could be incriminating."

Khan shrugged. "But why complicate matters by kidnapping a foreign national? It would be much simpler to kill you."

"Why are we wasting time discussing motive? These bastards have kidnapped a friend of mine, and I've come to you for help. It is your job, after all … "

Khan frowned. "I don't need to be reminded of my responsibilities, Mr Franklin, but I am a busy man. When I have come to you for assistance – always assuming you were to be found – all I got was evasion and a succession of half-truths, and yet when *you* want *my* help I am expected to drop everything ... "

Henry shrugged impatiently, but Khan had the bit between his teeth and wagged an accusing finger. "It's significant that I had no report from you the other day about the restaurant bombing – despite the promise to co-operate and keep me informed. We know you were there with your Israeli girl-friend."

Henry recalled what the hotel's assistant manager had said about rumours of Israeli involvement in the assassination of Dr Byoussi, and wondered if there was any significance in Khan's dig. The police inspector would not be directly concerned with the investigation into what was a political murder, but he would know what was going on; what the official view was.

Suddenly he no longer had the energy, or the will, to continue playing cat-and-mouse with someone whose help he needed. It was all very well for Beckton to lay down the law. Henry suppressed a snigger at the inadvertent pun, and decided to put most of his cards on the table. "Miss Kenan and I met by accident; we became friends, and on the day of the explosion we happened to have lunch together ... " He broke off, and corrected himself. "No, that's another of what you called 'half-truths'. She chose the restaurant because she had a contact in Rashid's organization, someone who promised to deliver some pretty startling information – the sort of evidence you were on about. Obviously, we were set-up. They tried to kill her – but we were lucky."

"Other people. innocent bystanders, were not so fortunate!"

"You can't blame us for that! You should know, Rashid doesn't care how many innocent people get hurt."

"That still does not explain why he should kidnap Miss Kenan when he could easily kill her – or kill you both?"

"I don't think Rashid is thinking logically," Henry suggested. "I think he's more concerned with settling a personal score." He recounted the events of the previous evening, and Khan listened in silence until he had finished.

"You are admitting that you broke into his office and opened a safe? You ... an academic who has never done anything more risky than negotiate a step ladder at the library?"

Henry ignored the sarcasm. "I did try to phone you. It was about midnight, and the call should have been logged."

Khan nodded. "It would have been; I shall check. Mind you, a message would have been more efficient; at least it would have been relayed to me at the first opportunity."

"I was scared of taking that risk."

"And you are suggesting that because his trap was sprung, it has become a vendetta to Rashid – that he wants to make you suffer ... ?"

"I'm sure of it," Henry insisted. "What is more, there was a witness to his humiliation. His pride wouldn't allow him to overlook what *I've* done to him – twice now ... "

"Twice?" Khan echoed, curiously. "It's beginning to make sense. I thought there would have to be something quite dramatic to force him to do things out of character ... ?"

Henry ignored the implied question. "Look, the place was in a shambles when I left ... one of the bookcases was knocked over. If we go there now you can see for yourself. The last person he'll be expecting is me, so we'll catch him off-guard."

Khan looked doubtful. "I wouldn't underestimate Rashid."

"Nor would I, but we are playing for high stakes. I'm

convinced it was his organization behind the murder of Doctor Byoussi ... "

Khan shrugged. "You are not the only person who subscribes to the theory. But as I said to you once before, it is another matter to prove such allegations."

"With all due respect, you won't prove anything by sitting on your backsides."

The inspector scowled. "The people investigating the assassination are working round the clock, I can assure you."

"I'm sorry, I'm sure they are. But what have you got to lose by indulging me?"

"As a public servant I have to be very circumspect. I can't march in on an ostensibly respectable newspaper editor – making wild accusations of kidnap."

"What is wrong with the truth – that you are merely trying to set my mind at rest. In other words, any excuse will do to get in, and then we can play it by ear ... "

At the editorial offices of Rashid's newspaper, it seemed strange using the proper entrance, but Henry was still too consumed with anger and concern for Ruti's safety, to dwell on the incongruity of the situation.

They were met by a pretty receptionist who asked them to wait for a moment while she checked whether the editor was available, but almost at once she returned smiling to show them into his private office. The room had burned a sharp image in Henry's memory, and in daylight it looked little different – except that the damaged bookcase had already been replaced by a new one.

Rashid got up from his desk to greet them, and advanced towards Inspector Khan, his right arm outstretched. To Henry's annoyance, the policeman accepted the handshake in friendly enough fashion, and the two exchanged diplomatic pleasantries. Then Rashid made a point of remembering his manners and, still addressing Khan, turned towards the Englishman and added: "I don't think I've had the pleasure of meeting your companion ... "

Henry managed to hold his temper in check, but he had to grit his teeth to answer politely enough: "We met last night ... "

Rashid looked at him in apparent consternation. "Last night ... ?"

Sensing that Henry was on the verge of violence, Khan stepped between them hurriedly, and remarked mildly: "Mr Franklin seems to think that you can throw some light on the disappearance of a friend of his, a Miss Kenan ... ?"

Rashid shook his head dazedly. "I am afraid I don't understand, Inspector. I presume you've come because I have a newspaper ... ? If that's so, I am sorry to say that we do not publish news of that description. Missing people do not interest our readers, I am afraid – this is a political journal."

The delicate thread of self-control suddenly snapped, and Henry leapt towards Rashid, grabbing him by the lapels of his suit, and hoisting him up on to his toes. "You filthy bastard – I'll kill you."

Twelve hours earlier, Rashid had been genuinely frightened for a few seconds, but now he was patently simulating terror, and Henry knew that behind that mask he was laughing at them. Protesting at the Englishman's "outrageous" assault, Rashid threatened to press charges unless he was released instantly, and Khan stepped in quickly and pulled Henry away. But despite the fact that he was still trembling with fury, Henry realized that he was getting nowhere, and that Khan was helpless to assist him at this stage.

As they left, Rashid was fastidiously straightening his

jacket. At the door Henry looked over his shoulder and caught a look of blatant triumph.

Only one avenue remained for Henry to explore – the *Cage D'Or*, and he would have to wait until nightfall before tackling it. A six-hour chasm of inactivity was as much as his frayed nerves would stand, and reluctantly he decided to try and catch up on some sleep. In his room again, after undressing and drawing the blinds, he stretched out on the bed and closed his eyes determinedly, and although his mind was a helter-skelter of confused thoughts, fatigue took hold and he drifted into sleep.

He woke sluggishly at seven o'clock, but a cool bath revived him and he was soon impatient for action. He felt strangely uplifted, as though the physical freshness had helped him mentally. He dressed methodically, substituting a pair of rubber-soled shoes for his normal pair, and putting a pair of leather gloves in his pocket. After only a momentary hesitation he also took Hassan's Beretta; he doubted whether he was capable of using it, but it might provide a degree of moral support. He slipped it into his inside breast pocket.

It was approaching nine o'clock when Henry left for the *Cage D'Or*, and he approached in the same manner as the previous visit – leaving the car on the main highway and going on foot, concealed for the most part by the trees. But this time he circled the club, looking for a first floor window that might lead directly to the room belonging to the hostess, Helga. After a few minutes he gave up in disgust – there were several that might have led to her room, and he did not want to disturb any of the other girls if it could be avoided – the fewer people implicated, the less the hazard.

At the side of the building, however, he found a narrow window which he suspected opened into a corridor. About

25 feet from the ground, it was a metal frame, casement window which opened outwards, and one of the casements was slightly ajar. The only means of access, apart from a ladder, was a drainpipe which ran up the side of the building – a distance of about six feet from the edge of the window sill. It was a long shot even for Henry's gangling physique, but he was determined to try it before resorting to one of the more easily gained bedroom windows. Having ensured there was no-one approaching, he put on the thin leather driving gloves to protect his hands against the brickwork.

The pipe itself was no problem; despite his initial awkwardness he shinned up it easily enough. But it was when he reached the level of the window that the real test presented itself. With his right hand he clung to the drainpipe, as well as gripping it tightly between his legs, and gradually eased his body against the face of the wall – reaching with his finger-tips of his left hand for the sill. Even in that spread-eagled position he was still about a foot or so away.

As the strain on his muscles began to tell, he suddenly recalled Khan's sarcastic remark about using a ladder to reach library books on the upper shelves, and how dramatically his lifestyle had changed in such a short period. But there was too much at stake for him to hesitate now. Dragging up his feet so that he was almost squatting against the wall, he braced his thighs, pushed hard against the pipe and leapt sideways for the sill. He managed to cover the gap but his clutching fingers could not retain their precarious hold, and he fell. In mid-air he managed to twist his body round so that he was no longer facing the wall and could judge his landing more easily. Luckily the ground was quite soft and at the moment of impact he managed to roll over, getting to his feet none the worse, except for a throbbing pain in the tips of the fingers of his left hand.

With a fairly good idea of how his error of judgement

could be rectified, he climbed up again. This time he sheered outwards, away from the wall, so that the movement was less restricted, and then at the peak of his impetus, grabbed at the sill, held fast, and quickly brought over his right arm to share the strain. Transferring his weight to the right, he put his other hand inside the window that was open a few inches, and loosened the metal bar which controlled its movement. Then with the same hand, he swung the casement outwards, over his lowered head. All he had to do then was to gain a better grip on the inside of the window with his left hand, shift his right over as well, and haul himself up and through.

Only when he was inside the deserted corridor did he notice the tremendous strain he had imposed on his arms. Both limbs, feeling as though they were swollen to twice their normal size, began to tremble violently, so that he had to rest for several minutes until they had recovered. He needed to wait for a much longer period for his muscles to recuperate adequately but he did not want to remain in the corridor for any length of time before getting to Helga's room. He padded along silently until he recognized the door, and then knelt down to look through the keyhole. However, the latch on the other side obscured his view. Gently he tried the handle – but the door was locked.

Gripping the gun in his right pocket, he tapped gently on the door and when there was no reply, he realized that Helga must still be in the main club in search of a client. If he broke into the room now, there was a chance that when she did arrive she would notice the lock had been tampered with. Wanting to catch her off-guard if possible, he decided to wait outside, around a bend in the corridor where it led to a spiral fire escape. He mentally crossed his fingers that none of the other girls should come up first – at least to this part of the passageway, in which case he would have to pose as a slightly furtive satisfied customer on his way out. Fortunately, luck was still with him. If anything, he was glad of the opportunity to rest his arms and legs until the muscles returned to normal.

He waited an interminable twenty minutes before Helga appeared with a middle-aged European in tow. She was wearing the same dress as she had the previous night, which somehow took an edge off her glamour, but as she bent to insert the key in the lock, she kept up a chattering commentary which her pleasant-enough looking companion seemed to find amusing. Henry took the gun out of his pocket, and as she opened the door he stepped from his hiding-place and ushered them both inside. The man who might have been on a business trip to Karachi and seeking an uncomplicated "night-out", was alarmed at the sight of the gun, but Helga although evidently not prepared to take any risks, merely looked amused. She sauntered into the room, threw her evening bag on the bed, and remarked: "Why you have gun? You cannot wait?"

Ignoring her for the moment, Henry addressed the man, trusting he understood English. "I've got some private business to transact. Get into the toilet ... " he said, indicating the door, " ... and don't make a sound – if you want to stay alive."

Nervous as he was, the man protested: "This is nothing to do with me – please let me go. I'll leave the club immediately, I promise!"

Henry shook his head. "I'm sorry – I know you're just a bystander, but I can't take the risk. If you do as you're told, you'll walk out of here in due course, none the worse – and with a full wallet! If you suddenly feel brave in there, spare a thought for your family; think of the shame you'd bring on them by getting shot in a Karachi brothel."

Helga's unfortunate client did as he was instructed and

Henry placed the back of a chair under the handle of the door, shutting him in. Then he turned to the smiling girl, and before he could stop himself, slapped her across the side of her face with the full weight of his arm and shoulder behind it. The force of the blow sent her staggering, and the smile was instantly transformed into a scowl.

Henry was conscious of his lower jaw sagging. He was as shocked as her by what had happened; it was as though John Hamilton, never allowed to leave the wings, had suddenly taken control. For a split second he was tempted to apologize, but her sullen reaction prompted him not to confuse the issue.

Grimacing with a mixture of pain and shock, she protested: "I am doing what they say! It's no my fault ... "

Despite his uneasiness, Henry found it difficult not to be amused by her excruciating grammar, and he said: "No need to apologize. I met you more than halfway."

Regaining her nerve, Helga nodded. "You said it, English! You think Helga will fall for you long streak of pork?"

"Bacon," he corrected. "I told you I'm not a policeman. Look, I'm not holding an inquest on last night – that's in the past. I'm prepared to give you an even break if you'll be honest with me for once. Last night your boss kidnapped a friend of mine ... "

" ... Well, you are not finding her here ... "

Henry put the gun away and grabbed her by the wrist, squeezing the bone so that she cried out. When he continued talking, the tone was deceptively soft, but it did not need a particularly observant person to notice that his anger was swimming close to the surface. "I was taking a gamble," he intoned. "Rashid could have a dozen hide-outs scattered about, but I came here because it was the only lead. Now you've saved me a lot of spadework – the fact that you know it was a woman, means that you've either seen her, or you've heard someone talking about it. Well, which is it?"

The girl maintained her sullen silence and he shook her by the shoulders roughly. "I'm not playing with words, Helga. I'm going to find out if it means breaking every bone in your body."

His subconscious winced at the cliché, and as he had feared, she laughed mockingly.

"I think the Englishman is gentleman," she replied. "How you say ... Not *cricket?* Yes that is right – it will not be cricket to beat up defenceless ladies."

Henry was desperate. He needed to break down her resistance yet he realized subtlety was not enough. Averting his eyes, he doubled her up with a punch to the solar plexus, retaining his grip on her wrist so that she could not fall to the ground. He waited anxiously for her to beg for mercy, but when she had finally regained her breath, she was just as defiant: "Go to hell!" she screamed.

Without comment he dragged her over to the dressing-table, rifled the drawers until he found a pair of scissors and then, forcing her to face the mirror, he held them up threateningly, and whispered menacingly: "Perhaps your face means more to you than a scrap of information ... "

It was his final bluff, and it nearly misfired. As the point of the scissors moved slowly towards her face, she struggled desperately to free herself, and with a hysterical note of bravado, she panted: "I *dare* you!" But he continued the movement remorselessly and as the steel touched her face and began to strain against the drawn flesh, her nerve broke at last – only an instant before his.

"She is staying at a warehouse in the city."

Henry stepped back and slid the scissors out of reach under the bed. Taking her wrist he said: "You'll come with me this time – I'm leaving nothing to chance."

"But I am not knowing where, on my mother's life!"
Helga protested.

He grinned without humour. "Then you'll have to help
me find it. You know, there is just one thing you told me last
night that still impresses me as the truth – the fact that you
love money! Before we go I'm going to find me some added
security."

Dragging her with him he began to systematically ransack
the room, starting with the drawers and cupboards and
finishing with the bed. It took him about ten minutes but his
persistence was rewarded: inside a pillow case he found four
separate wads of bank-notes in different currencies – worth,
at a calculated guess, little short of two thousand pounds.
He put the bundles in his jacket pockets. "If you're
double-crossing me again, I'll destroy your little nest-egg,"
he announced.

With the fate of her precious savings in the balance,
Helga's morale disintegrated completely, and she begged
him not to take the money. But this time Henry was not
relinquishing the initiative, and pulling her towards the
door, he said: "Come on – we've got a long drive ahead."
Only now did Helga admit defeat, and she began to sob
quietly. Then while he waited for her to calm down, she
said: "I lie to you – she is here at club!"

Half suspecting the truth, Henry asked her to be more
precise.

"Just along corridor – near where you hiding for me."

"Is it a room like this?"

"Yes, the same. It belonging to one of girls."

"What about guards ... ?" he demanded.

Helga dabbed her cheeks dry with a handkerchief and
looked in a hand mirror, conscious of her appearance even
in the midst of her troubles. She appeared to think for a
moment, and then said: "One man is there all the time,

although sometimes he plays cards with friend. I was not sure."

Trusting that she was now too dispirited to lie, he made his plans quickly. Taking the gun from his pocket, he pointed to the bedclothes and told her to fold the two sheets into strips and knot the ends together. While she was carrying out his instructions he backed warily to the bathroom door, removed the chair and looked in at the man inside. "You've been very quiet," he informed him, "and now I'm going outside for ten minutes or so. In a quarter of an hour you can leave – just open the door and walk out. I shall be busy in the corridor outside and if you come out too soon, I'll shoot you … "

The man nodded nervously, and after shutting the door Henry told Helga, who had finished knotting the sheets, to tie the makeshift "rope" around his waist. Then he forced her to stand in front of him and told her: "You'll do all the talking. Knock on the door and when the guard answers, tell him you've got a message from the boss – or say anything that will get him to open up. I'll do the rest – and you'd better stay close to me if you want that money back."

He was soon to realize with a sense of frustration that he waited twenty minutes only a few feet from the same door, ignorant of the fact that Ruti was inside. As Helga knocked and asked to be let in, he tensed himself for the rush, and when the door opened slightly he charged against it with his shoulder, carrying Helga with him, and bowling over the man on the other side. The edge of the door had caught the guard a violent blow down one side of the face and as he staggered back in pain, Henry leapt after him and clubbed him several times with the gun until he collapsed.

The attack had been so sudden that the man's gun was still in its shoulder holster. Henry removed it and put it in his own pocket.

The room, as Helga had predicted, was similar to her own, and he was only a couple of steps from the bed on which Ruti was lying, asleep or unconscious. Shutting the door behind him and positioning Helga where he could see her, he bent over Ruti and felt her pulse. She was wearing a summer frock, leaving parts of her chest and shoulders, and her arms, bare and he could see no signs of violence. Her pulse was normal too and Helga confirmed his suspicion by remarking: "She will be all right – only drugged."

He picked Ruti up in his arms, and instructing Helga to walk in front, made for the corridor window from which he had entered. Then gently laying the unconscious girl on the floor, he unwound the sheet from his body and told Helga to tie one end to a radiator against the wall.

"Make sure it holds because you'll be going down first!" he warned.

Helga carried out his instructions and reluctantly clambered over the sill and down the makeshift rope. When she was out of the window, Henry lifted Ruti and draping her over his shoulder in a fireman's lift, prepared to follow. He waited until Helga had reached the bottom and then went over the edge himself. On firm ground again he wasted no time and hurried through the trees to his car on the main highway. He laid Ruti on the back seat and told Helga to get in beside him. When she refused, he shrugged and switched on the ignition. "That's all right with me – I'll put your money in the post – *if* I can remember. If you prefer not to take any chances, come with us and I'll drop you about a mile down the road. All I want is a head start before you can get back and raise the alarm."

A few minutes later he returned her savings which, for want of an evening bag, she slipped down the front of her dress, and cursing him fluently in a mixture of German, English and Urdu she began her ill-equipped hike back to the club.

At the back of the car Ruti was beginning to stir, and with mounting relief he knew she was in no danger. The first step, he decided, was to get her back to the hotel, where she could be seen by a doctor.

By the time they arrived in the centre of Karachi the stream of cool air entering the car windows had revived her sufficiently for her to sit up, and when she found her bearings, he explained what had happened. Leaning a little unsteadily on his arm, she was able to walk into the hotel. To his surprise, although she had been unconscious for several hours, it was sleep she seemed to need, and by the morning she had fully recovered.

Nine

By the time their relationship had been consummated, Henry suspected he was in love. He was overjoyed yet somewhat bewildered to discover that Ruti appeared to reciprocate his feelings. He could not help wondering if it was too good to be true; if there was still not some insurmountable problem capable of throwing a spanner in the works. Living among people to whom deception was second nature, he could not escape the sneaking suspicion that Ruti was making up to him for some reason he had not yet been able to fathom.

Yet despite this anxiety he had a gut reaction that it was no act; that her reactions of the past hour or so after her long sleep had been instinctive and genuine. And when he told her the truth about himself – although it was still far simpler to maintain the pretence of having been recruited by D16 for a 'one-off' assignment – he knew that his real background could not be of any interest to Israeli Intelligence.

"It explains why you are so different to other men I have known," Ruti conceded. "You are just as courageous ... more so to me ... but you are missing the ruthless streak. It reminds me how much I have changed – and not for the better. Henry, what are we going to do about us?"

He leaned over in bed and kissed the tip of her nose. "The

most important thing from now on is to be together," he said, "and that means getting away – back to the real world ... "

"But this *is* the real world," she pointed out.

"If that's true and *mine* was the dream world, then that is where I want to return. I want life to be ordinary again and escape from this nightmare. Can *you* get away? Will they let you?"

"I don't know." She looked at him with concern. "What about you?"

"I should think D16, or whoever they are, will be relieved to get rid of me. For me, it's only the start of the problem. You and I come from different worlds and we've got to find common ground. The only thing I know is books. I doubt if I could make a living in your country. How do you feel about coming to England?"

"How could I stand the weather?" she asked. She shivered and pulled the sheet up to her neck.

"You'll have my love to keep you warm," he said, kissing her again. He got out of bed and began to get dressed. "Look, whatever we decide, we can't just pack our bags and leave – especially you. I'll stay in Karachi for as long as it takes, but from now on I'm giving Rashid a wide berth. From this minute I'm going to behave like a tourist ... "

She patted the space he had just vacated. "Do you have to start *this* minute?"

The warmth of the bed and the girl he loved looked tempting, but he shook his head. "It's a question of priorities," he pointed out. "Having said I'm going to do my best to forget Rashid, *he* may not be so forgiving. He has a number of scores to settle, so I'm off now to see Inspector Khan. I'm going to tell him everything ... at least, almost everything. The more ammunition I can give him the better. Make yourself at home."

"No thanks, I've also got things to do," she protested, climbing out of bed. Their eyes met for a moment, and seeing the look of wonderment on his face she blushed, and moved into his arms so that he could not see her nakedness. "Don't look," she whispered.

"You're *shy?*" he asked, incredulous.

She giggled. "It's never bothered me before because I have never cared about anyone. Besides, no-one ever thought I was perfection. You do ... "

"I don't ... "

"You *don't?!*"

"Of course I do."

"Well, I'm not and I don't want you to see where my bosom sags, and ... "

"They don't," he insisted, pushing her to arm's length as though to prove the point. "*There*. I'm right."

She wriggled free of his clutches, and snorted disbelievingly: "They say love is blind. I'm going to have a quick shower."

"Why don't I join you?"

"Why don't you?"

Henry was sorely tempted, and he knew they were in danger and would feel better when he had put Khan in the picture. "Later," he promised, "and then every day for the rest of our lives ... "

"When we are old and grey?"

"Till death do us part! Meanwhile, getting back to the present, where shall we meet?"

She reflected. "I have a few telephone calls to make. Can I make them here?" When he nodded, she continued: "I might have to wait for a while if some of those people are not immediately available. Then I have some shopping to do, so let's say at my flat." She gave him an address off Shar-E-Faisal. "I should be there for the afternoon."

In explaining his change of heart, Henry was frank with Inspector Khan. He left little out, apart from his links with Beckton and his suspicions that Crawford was a double agent, considering that to be an internal matter. "Now I feel I can get out of your hair with a clear conscience," he concluded.

Khan laughed. "I shall miss you, Mr Librarian. When is your flight to London?"

Henry hesitated. "I haven't actually booked yet. I thought I would catch up on the sightseeing for a few days. I'm supposed to be an expert on manuscripts, and yet I haven't even been to the National Museum, where there are supposed to be around ten thousand specimens – and that's within walking distance of the hotel. Apart from what I have to do, I'm also hoping that Miss Kenan might come back to England with me."

"You know, of course, that the young lady works for Israeli Intelligence?"

"All that concerns me, Inspector, is that one day she might be a librarian's wife."

"Meanwhile, while she remains in this country her life is in danger – and so is yours."

"We shall be careful."

"So you are committed to stay?"

"Only for as long as it is necessary. I intend to keep my nose clean from now on, and in return I'm hoping for a degree of police protection."

"That can be arranged, Mr Franklin, but there are problems ... "

"Problems ... ?"

"You must know that we turn a blind eye to the activities of Intelligence agents from other countries. Of course, if they misbehave themselves we crack down on them; at least we deport them. But for most of the time we have to treat them with the respect accorded to foreign nationals – that is, we have to use our discretion. However, we do not extend to them what might be called 'protection' – and nor do they wish or expect it. In the circumstances, although you may not be an agent, the rule applies to you as well as Miss Kenan ... "

"But it can be arranged, you said ... "

"What is that odd expression you use? 'You scratch my backside and I'll scratch yours'?"

"*Back* – not backside," Henry corrected. "What sort of itch do you have in mind?"

"I would like to make use of your services – just this once."

"Something to do with books?"

Khan made no effort to conceal his exasperation. "You say you've been to Rashid's villa. That's a pleasure we have not yet had. The trouble is that on the few occasions when Rashid leaves the place, it's usually surrounded by guards who live in a guest lodge in the grounds. He calls them students, but we know better, of course."

"I can remember the place and some of the guards, but I've no idea where it is ... "

Khan laughed. "That is something we know, at least. It is a very secluded spot – probably why he chose it – by the sea to the south of Keamari. We have finally found a way to get him and his personal bodyguard away, which just leaves the men in the grounds. The problem is who to send ... "

"Why should that be a problem?"

"Oh, I've got several men who are capable enough, but if the plan should misfire the scandal would be enormous – police officer breaking into the home of a respected newspaper editor."

Henry laughed nervously, suspecting what Khan was getting at. "But why use your men? There must be any number of criminals who would help out for a favour in return."

"Of course, but we are not after money or valuables. The sort of petty crook you are talking about would not understand what we are looking for, even if we *could* trust him not to double-cross us."

"So you thought of me? But surely the sort of scandal that scares you so much would be nothing compared to that if a foreigner was caught ... "

"It is not the same. You see, this is not a police operation. We are working with the people investigating the Byoussi murder, and they have special powers. I can assure you that at the merest whiff of an international scandal, you would be back in England, safe and sound, before you could catch your breath."

"But I don't want to be back there without Miss Kenan."

"That could be arranged too."

"If they have so much power, why can't they do the break-in themselves?"

Khan shrugged. "They could, but *I* promised that *we* would do it."

"*We?*"

"Karachi is my territory. Moysin Serai, the man in charge, is an old school chum of mine. We have helped each other before, and this time it was my opportunity."

"So why the change of heart?"

"You misunderstand me, Mr Franklin. The operation is my responsibility, and I intend to carry it out – one way or another. It did not enter my head to involve you until you marched in a few moments ago and presented me with what seemed like a heaven-sent opportunity. You are at liberty to refuse, of course – that is your prerogative ... but ... "

"But ... ?" Henry anticipated him.

"You could find that we are too short-staffed in the next

few days to provide the sort of protection you were asking for ... But why should you refuse? You hate Rashid as much as we do, and besides, the job is right up your street."

"Don't start that all over again. I thought you believed me at last!"

"Whatever I believe is immaterial," Khan retorted, irritably. "It didn't stop you breaking into the man's office!"

Henry groaned. Would no-one ever believe him? But reluctant as he was to become involved again, it occurred to him that it might even be safer taking the ball into Rashid's court, than waiting for him to come after them. Perhaps Ruti would accompany him, providing the expertise he lacked.

Weakening, he asked how they could be sure Rashid would be away to fit in with their plans so conveniently.

"I can only reveal that if I have your agreement to work with us ... ?"

"I'll work with you if I have guarantee that Miss Kenan and I will be *protected* – got out of the country if things go wrong."

"You have my word."

"Then you can count me in. What's the plan?"

"Have you heard of someone called Sabiya Byoussi?"

"No, but from the name, I suppose she is a relative of the President?"

"His only daughter."

"Come to think of it, the name is familiar. Could I have seen her on TV in England?"

"Probably. She's young, highly intelligent and has quite a following, particularly among women, so that her views count for something. Luckily, Serai's nephew is a friend of hers from their university days, so he has a better relationship with her than might be expected of most security officials. He told her why he suspected Rashid, and asked for her help ... "

"Why *do* you suspect Rashid?" Henry interjected. "I know why *I* do, but presumably there is no concrete evidence, so it has to be more than an inspired hunch ... "

"Behaviour patterns – something we discussed at our first meeting. Doctor Byoussi was so popular that his assassin would have to be a crank, motivated by personal hatred – but madmen do not plan assassinations. They rush out of crowds with a knife or gun; invariably they get caught in the act. This bombing was carefully organized – and that brings us back to motive, and the killer's intention ... "

"I thought about that," said Henry. "It could have been to rally support against what might be regarded as a common enemy ... Israel, or the CIA ... American mercenaries, as they're usually called."

Khan nodded. "You got the first half right. The rumour in the bazaars is that the bomb was planted by agents from India or Bangladesh. Many people are still bitter over losing what they still regard as East Pakistan. A new hate campaign puts fire into faint hearts ... "

" ... and makes them forget empty bellies."

"Except that we must not overlook the significance of Doctor Byoussi's popularity. Assassinations have become commonplace in the world today ... in fact, we were in at the beginning. Remember, our first prime minister, Liaquat Ali Khan was killed in 1951 – but it was a typically pointless murder, and his enemies achieved nothing. But Byoussi had *no* enemies – least of all, Rashid, if you accept his public image of being a nationalist, only slightly right of centre. Of course he claims to be outraged, but for every moderate who moves to the right on occasions like this, another already on the right completes the swing and becomes a fanatic. He benefits at both levels."

"How short-sighted can people be?"

"I am not so quick to condemn. Everyone is ignorant until he knows the facts."

"We don't always have to know; to suspect should be enough. I am automatically suspicious of politicians and diplomats ... "

"Automatically?"

"By definition. What *is* diplomacy in peacetime – other than a respectable cloak for intrigue? It may still conjure up images of gentlemen in honourable face-to-face discussions, but that sort of thing disappeared when Chamberlain came back from Germany in 1939 with Hitler's piece of paper. Today, friendly powers spy on each other – let alone the so-called enemy. The only difference is that politicians generally draw the line at blood – people like Rashid regard it as part of the price to be paid."

Khan nodded. "Then you will be impressed with our Machiavellian little plot. Rashid believes he has infiltrated Serai's department; he does not realize that Serai lets him have odd bits of intelligence from time to time, in the hope that when it suits us he can deliberately feed Rashid false information."

Henry thought of Crawford and wondered if Beckton had agreed to a similar arrangement.

" ... With Sabiya Byoussi's permission, Serai let it be known that she is terribly embittered by her father's murder; that she accepts the theory India or Bangladesh was behind the plot. In short, to give the impression that she supports many of her father's early views on the validity of the Muslim cause – the fairly right-wing philosophy he used to expound, before age and responsibility mellowed him."

"I hadn't realized that Doctor Byoussi was a nationalist?"

"In common with many of our political leaders who were more extreme in their youth, Byoussi moved more and more towards the centre. But the rhetoric still sounds as impressive, and from a dynamic younger person like Sabiya, even more so. Rashid's group represents various shades of nationalism and for him it makes her a potential member of his splinter group on the far right – the political as opposed to the terrorist wing. He desperately needs new recruits from the so-called intelligentsia."

"You mean that Serai gambled on the chance that Rashid might make a play for her?"

"And that the thought of support from the daughter of the man he murdered would appeal to his macabre sense of humour," said Khan. "Through a mutual friend, Rashid suggested that Sabiya might contribute an article for his newspaper. Unfortunately Miss Byoussi had arranged to go abroad for three or four months, but Serai persuaded her that we could not miss the opportunity, and to telephone Rashid. She said that she would be pleased to discuss the project, but that if he wanted something topical he would have to come and visit her today – the last free day she would have before leaving."

"Come and see *her*?"

"It is a measure of the significance of such an article that he was prepared to cancel his diary engagements for today and fly up to Islamabad in time for lunch."

"That means he can be back by tonight – it doesn't give us much time."

"It is a risk we must take," Khan pointed out. "We can't get into the house by daylight because of Rashid's men hovering about the grounds. On the other hand you have to remember that Sabiya Byoussi is not only a person of some importance but an attractive woman. He should be quite flattered by the invitation."

"How long would he be there?"

"I can only guess, but the general idea is that she would

invite a few friends to lunch, where the conversation would be general. The more serious *tête-a-tête* would be later and she would endeavour to arrange dinner for a slightly awkward time – to make it difficult for him to catch the last flight back to Karachi. It is possible to get back by car, of course, but it is a tiring journey, and it would be much simpler to stay the night. However, to be on the safe side, you must get in and out again as soon as possible."

To his surprise the discussion with Inspector Khan had lasted little more than half-an-hour, and Henry took a chance on Ruti still being at the hotel. He was in luck.

Ruti was amused by his change of plan, conceding that it was an opportunity not to be missed, but she pulled his leg over helping the police. "What was that expression you used? Escaping from a nightmare?" she chided.

"All I remember saying is that you and I should stay together – which means that I'm stuck in Karachi until your people decide to let you go. So long as I'm here I may as well do something useful, and since I don't like being separated from you any longer than necessary, why don't you come along to keep me company?"

"To ride 'shotgun'?"

"Hopefully we shall be in and out without being spotted, but I'd feel happier with you to hold my hand. Shall we meet at your flat?"

"Do you still have the car you hired?" she asked. "You can go in mine, but if I'm held up we could meet there."

He explained the need to start as soon as it got dark. "Apart from that, I'm easy."

"I'm waiting for one more call, and then I can leave. Let's try to meet at my flat in an hour or so. If I am not there, either wait, or try me here again in case I have been held up."

When Henry parked the car there was still time to kill so he had a snack in an open-air restaurant and then took a leisurely stroll in the sunshine. He was walking in the direction of the older part of the city, where modern buildings such as Broadcasting House, were fewer, and the character of the street changed quite suddenly. Now he was in what appeared to be a street market, except that it was different to any he had seen. The trade here was not only traditional but he was surprised to see a dentist operating almost shoulder-to-shoulder with a hairdresser; and, much busier, a fortune teller and alongside him a faith healer, both with a patient queue. Henry would have liked to watch the healer, but his vibrations must have been unharmonious because the man gestured to him to clear off.

Henry took the hint and wandered back to the more modern shops, wondering if he should take back a few small presents to his staff at the library, and Heather. His stomach fell away at the prospect of trying to explain things – not only to Heather, but to his parents. Perhaps they had been right all along in wondering what she saw in him, so perhaps it would not come as quite such a shock. She would be better off with someone a little more ambitious than him. He tried to visualize her with a caricature of what he imagined to be a dynamic young executive, and surprisingly the picture was disturbing. True, she had never set his blood racing as Ruti did, but Heather was also a good friend – probably the best friend he had.

He forced himself to concentrate on the shop window and recalled that no-one at the library was supposed to know he was even out of the country, so that exotic leatherware, oriental scarves and jewellery might come as something of a shock – one that Beckton would not appreciate.

The flat was above the next parade of shops, the entrance in a side alley. It was not much more than thirty years old and actually had a lift which he took to the second floor. He was about to ring the bell, when he realized that the door was ajar. Ruti had presumably beaten him to it, leaving the door open so that he could get in while she – hopefully – was taking a shower. The flat was surprisingly large, the door opening on to a long passageway, off which were several rooms. Disappointingly there was no running water to be heard, nor the sound of a cistern filling, so he called out, and when there was no reply he opened several of the doors in turn expecting to find her hiding – but the flat was empty.

By now surprise had turned to anxiety. It was just possible that she had dashed down to the shops, but it seemed highly unlikely that a person of her background and training would leave the door on the latch, even though she was expecting someone. But he did not need to worry for long – a phone call established that she was still at the Balimar. It was her turn to be concerned. "*I* didn't leave the door unlocked," she insisted. "Someone must have broken in."

"Searching for something?"

" … Or planting a bomb. Be very careful, Henry!"

"Don't panic. If it is a bomb, it would probably be timed to go off when you're most likely to be here. If I see anything at all suspicious I'll contact Inspector Khan. If not, you can still play safe by staying the night with me at the hotel." Even as he was speaking he realized that it could just as easily be a booby-trap, triggered to detonate when a drawer or cupboard was opened, but not wishing to alarm her he said nothing.

"I'll come there," she announced.

"No. If there *is* anything hidden I'll find it by the time you get here. In any case, this is in the opposite direction to Rashid's villa, so it seems pointless coming all the way here, only to go back again. I'll give it another half-hour at the flat and then I'll make tracks."

"Be careful, darling."

"Don't worry, I will."

"Where shall we rendezvous?"

He tried to visualize the villa but only had a hazy recollection. "All I remember is that it was quite isolated, so we had better not take the cars too near in case we're spotted. I suggest we both make for the house; it might be practical to go straight in – unless it turns out to be built like a fortress. You play it by ear."

"Be careful," she repeated.

Heartened by her concern for him, Henry forgot his apprehension as he started with the easiest rooms – bathroom, toilet and kitchen. He had only the faintest idea of what a bomb looked like, but anything that seemed in the slightest unusual would be justification enough for phoning the police. He was about to start on the lounge, when he thought he heard a faint scraping noise from the only room he had not tried because the door was locked. He froze in his tracks, and his pulse started to quicken. For several seconds he was uncertain as what to do – whether to wait behind the door and hope that he could ambush the intruder, or to take some more positive action in case there was another exit he did not know about. He tried looking through the keyhole, but the view was obscured. Gingerly he tried the handle again, but it was definitely locked.

He cursed himself for being so unobservant as he suddenly spotted something he had overlooked: all the doors in the flat were surmounted by hinged glass panels, presumably to improve the ventilation because all were in the open position. Silently he took a chair and stood on the seat to look into the room. It was obviously Ruti's bedroom. The intruder was a man, although all he could make out was a silhouette, back to him, bending over a suitcase on a bed. Typically, he had left the Beretta and the captured automatic at the hotel, so he could not rely on bluff. Without one it was impossible to get into the room ... nor was it possible to stay where he was.

But bluff was still the name of his game. Relying on the distance between them to restrict the intruder's view, he took the fountain pen from his inside breast pocket and held it on the window frame, aiming it like a revolver with the barrel partially concealed by his cheek. Looking along its length, as though taking careful aim, he called out: "Put your hands up, please, or I'll put a bullet in your back."

He kept his voice low but in the stillness it sounded frighteningly loud and the man jumped. Then slowly he turned round and Henry recognized Colonel Crawford. The shock of seeing the bland, fish-like face was so great that the hand gripping his make-believe gun relaxed, and he almost dropped it. All he could think of to say was a tame: "What are *you* doing here?"

Not the slightest embarrassed by his predicament, Crawford was snappish. "Wasting my time, it seems, since you seem to have woken up at last to your responsibilities. I'm a desk man – obviously not cut out for this sort of thing ... " His manner was so true to character that Henry momentarily hesitated, but logic reasserted itself.

"That's not an answer, Colonel Crawford. I can see what you're doing; I want to know why?"

"Why? For heaven's sake, I should have thought that was obvious! If it's not, then what are you doing here?"

"Waiting for an answer!"

Crawford sighed. "Intelligence means knowing what is going on – not just what the Pakis are doing, but every Tom, Dick and Harry. Beckton is particularly suspicious of the Israelis."

The air of self-righteousness added to Henry's sense of unreality, standing on a chair with a make-believe gun in his hand. To compensate, there was an edge to his voice as he ordered Crawford to come and unlock the door.

"Put that damn gun away," Crawford responded. "You don't think I'm going to start a shoot-out at my age?"

It was with a mixture of relief and confidence that he could cope with the older man physically if the need arose, that Henry put the pen back in his pocket, although to be sure he did not climb off the chair until Crawford had carried out the instruction.

Face to face at last, Crawford remained bad-tempered. "I don't know what to make of you, Franklin. One minute you're trying to play the innocent, the next you're being officious and checking up on me with London. If you've come to search this place, that's fine with me – but I take exception when one of Beckton's people draws a gun on me merely for doing what he should have done days ago ... "

"You just conceded you were a desk man. When I found someone here, it could have been anyone. Besides, didn't you hear my voice on the phone just now?"

"Of course not! Yes, I heard *a* voice, but the sound was muffled, so I assumed it was one of the Israelis."

"How did you get in?" Henry demanded, conscious of his inexperience in these matters.

"I bribed the concierge. Said I was a friend who was expected ... She wouldn't hear of it at first, when I greased her palm she reverted to type. Not exactly the height of discretion on my part, I suppose, but I know nothing about breaking into flats – I haven't had your training."

Henry was too preoccupied to be aware of the irony of the situation; not trusting him, he was wondering how to handle Crawford. But short of attempting to beat the truth out of him – which was scarcely his scene – he was stuck for a solution.

It suddenly occurred to him he had nothing to lose by

taking the colonel along to Rashid's home. If the man from the embassy was genuine, as Beckton maintained, then he might be useful; if he was in the pay of Rashid Henry could at least keep tabs on him. Providing he did not let Crawford out of his sight, there was not much the older man could do to hinder the operation. If for any reason Crawford refused to help, he would be forced to overpower him, leaving him tied up in Ruti's flat – even if it meant abject apologies later.

" ... Not that I think you'll find anything ... " Crawford was saying. "I've been through this room with a toothcomb but I've found nothing of interest. Now I suppose you'll want to start all over again?"

"On the contrary," said Henry soothingly. "Beckton spoke very highly of you, so if you've conducted a search to your satisfaction there's no point in doubling up when we are pressed for time. If you really want to be helpful you can come with me – I'm expecting a break-through at last."

He gave Crawford a potted account of his plan to break into Rashid's villa while he was out of the city, but deciding not to reveal that he was working with the police and the national security agency. Crawford admitted he was impressed. "I take my hat off to you, Franklin. I don't know how you've pulled this off, and I don't expect you to tell me. In this business a man's contacts are his own affair. Perhaps you won't mind passing them on when you go back to London?"

"We'll see ... " Henry was relieved that although he must have realized there was an element of risk, Crawford had not tried to avoid accompanying him. Perhaps he had misjudged the man ...

Ten

To Ruti Kenan the future had never seemed so bleak. Depression was new to her, and she did not need to be told that it was essential to shake it off before reaching the villa. But she discovered that mind over matter was all very well in theory; in practise it was no easier to ignore than physical discomfort, like a severe stomach cramp – and no less debilitating. Although it seemed a fairly routine assignment, she had been taught never to take anything for granted; whatever the odds, she needed to be totally alert. In ordinary circumstances the pumping effect of the adrenalin would have been enough to clear her mind, but this time it was different. She could no more shut out discordant memories of the conversation she had just had, than she could pretend her life had not been turned upside down by Henry Franklin.

The conversation, via short-wave radio, had been with Avram Deutsch, her controller. In the two years she had worked under Deutsch, she had come to like and respect the man. Deutsch was looked up to by everyone; his operational judgement was impeccable, his actions decisive; the combination being reflected in his remarkable track record. Indeed, his department lived in constant dread that he was destined for the top and that sooner or later he could be replaced by someone falling considerably short of the standards he had set. In his late forties, Deutsch had spent a number of years in Germany and the United States, ostensibly in the diplomatic service, and he was considerably more cosmopolitan than the bulk of his colleagues. A bachelor, he had few interests outside his job, which might have accounted for his single-mindedness. It was said that he had only one weakness; he collected archaeological artefacts, and in that respect he was not always too particular about their origin.

Ruti had been attracted by Deutsch's natural unassuming authority, and there was a degree of intimacy between them – although nothing improper had ever taken place – yet she wished it did not have to be him to whom she would have to present her resignation. It was his perceptiveness she feared; she had no illusions over her ability to conceal her true reasons. In fact, she had tried to compromise by sounding him out initially on the general principle, but he was not taken-in by the deliberate vagueness.

Deutsch knew the men and women in his team. He did not need the various reports, psychological and aptitude tests that had been compiled to know that Ruti was not only good at her job, but utterly dedicated. Talk, even hypothetical talk, of opting out at the very start of a promising career, was uncharacteristic of the girl he had trained. He probed further, and when she hedged, he knew intuitively that it had something to do with the Englishman she had mentioned in her earlier reports. When she admitted the connection – doing her best to explain the way the relationship had developed through her abduction and rescue – he listened without comment for several minutes until she had finished.

"Very interesting," he remarked finally, unmoved. "But I don't get the connection between this incident and wanting to resign – unless it has something to do with losing your nerve?"

"Does it have to be anything as cut and dried as that?" she had protested, flustered by his manner. The difference was that she and Franklin were no longer strangers, she pointed out; that they had formed a relationship.

Deutsch admitted that he was disappointed in her; that he expected clinical, as opposed to emotional judgements from someone of her training and experience. Apart from a name, what did she know about this Englishman? What was his interest in her? Had it not occurred to her how relatively easy it had been to get her away from the *Cage D'Or?*

Ruti's heart sank. She knew Deutsch was too impersonal to be motivated by anything other than genuine suspicion, and who could blame him? She denied that her rescue had been stage-managed, pointing out that Mossad stood to gain more from Franklin's goodwill, than the other way about; the opportunity now to take a look at Rashid's papers was evidence enough.

The Controller remained unsympathetic. "I can't answer that," he said, "but in this business it is *enough* for me to be suspicious – and for you to be doubly cautious. It could be a trap."

"I trust Henry Franklin with my life."

"Then you are a fool. The only person you should trust is *me* – and even then I don't expect you to suspend judgement completely."

"That is a contradiction. You have just been saying that you are not prepared to accept my judgement – because you have decided I'm no longer able to think and behave rationally."

"That isn't a contradiction."

"I thought we had a rapport, you and I. Obviously I was deluding myself. If you don't trust me implicitly – enough to appreciate that I would never allow myself to make emotional judgements – then I cannot do my job properly any more. Surely that is reason enough for wanting to get out as soon as possible?"

"Don't be childish!" he retorted. "I am your boss, not your father, or a lover. Don't expect me to treat you as such. The job *has* to come first, but that doesn't mean that I don't care about you. Meanwhile, *you* have obligations ... it isn't any old job you are doing ... "

"I know that. If it *was*, there would be no problem. I could resign whenever I liked."

"You knew this when you joined."

"That it was irrevocable? I wasn't expecting a *life* sentence. It is not as though my head is full of state secrets. What if I was disabled in action, and had to give up? Or if I wanted to settle down and have children in the ordinary way?"

"He is prepared to settle in Israel, your man? What does D16 have to say about that? That could also be part of a plan ... "

"Henry is not with D16, or *any* Intelligence agency. Perhaps that is part of the attraction."

"And you *believe* that?" Deutsch's tone was incredulous.

"Is it *so* impossible, Avram? In any case, whatever he is, or may have been, it is all in the past. He loves me, and I love him."

"That, I am prepared to believe, but the odds could not be more stacked against you if Franklin belonged to the PLO. Talk about star-crossed lovers ... Romeo and Juliet had nothing on you two ... "

"I know what the odds are. We are scarcely teenagers."

"Look Ruti, give me time to find a replacement and you can come back and take some leave. If this guy Franklin keeps his nose clean – proves to our satisfaction he really has dropped out of the business – and you still feel the same way in six months, we'll talk again. Meanwhile tonight, your job comes first. Collaboration is fine as long as they are handing it out, but anything *you* discover you tell *me* first ... "

Heading towards Keamari, Ruti brooded over the conversation. Her initial impatience at the Controller's refusal to unbend was gradually replaced by resignation. In view of the circumstances of her meeting with Henry, she realized that Deutsch's concern was understandable. She genuinely believed that what she had told him was the truth; that she was capable of keeping her head – despite the fact that when she pictured Henry's face her stomach turned over. She recalled how they had first met; how dispassionately businesslike she had been then! How bemused he had seemed – on reflection, surely proof in itself that he was no agent.

Ruti was not inexperienced in relationships with men, although she had never been in love, apart from a brief infatuation with one of her professors at university. It was Henry's gentleness ... gentility? ... she was not too sure of the right word in English ... that made him so different. *Gentility* ... Gentile ... she wondered at her parent's reaction to the news that the man with whom she wanted to share her life was not a Jew. She smiled affectionately at the picture, confident that they were too enlightened to object, at least not on those grounds.

Consulting the map at regular intervals, she estimated she was just over a kilometre from the villa when she left the car and continued on foot. It seemed likely that she was ahead of Henry and since they had agreed not to hang about, she heeded Deutsch's advice, and take advantage of any time she had in her favour. There had not been time to ask what Inspector Khan hoped to find and that would influence what she subsequently decided to hand over, and what to keep for herself. Ten minutes later she was able to identify the villa from the size of the grounds. It was surrounded by a low wall, topped by iron railings. Cautiously she completed a reconnaissance of the perimeter, estimating that the property consisted of about two acres of cultivated woodland. The assortment of date, plum and orange trees were similar to those in her parents' garden at home, but from their numbers and the variety of sizes, she suspected they had been planted at different times; that the principal purpose was to screen the villa from the road. It was concealed even from the front entrance, and two single-storey white-stone cottages on either side of the drive leading down to the main gates, could have been mistaken for a Customs border post. There was no sign of life, but she guessed there were men inside, and others patrolling the grounds.

Satisfied, Ruti retraced her footsteps until she reached a particularly deserted spot. The railings presented no difficulty and she dropped silently onto a sandy soil, moving quickly into the trees. Relatively invisible she was able to take her time, making sure that her eyes had adjusted to the gloom, and that she did not lose her bearings. When she reached a clearing she stopped for several minutes trying to work out routes that might be followed by the guards. Her patience was rewarded when she spotted two of them patrolling the inner edge of the trees. They were on the other side of the house, about fifty metres away and, engrossed in an animated conversation, they would not have seen her. Even so she waited until they had passed. Staying parallel to them but moving in the opposite direction and still using the trees for cover she approached the villa, a large white stone building on two floors. When she was reasonably sure that she had not been spotted she sprinted across the remaining twenty metres of open ground to the final hazard, a wide gravel drive which magnified the sound of footsteps and which she had to negotiate with the utmost care.

The house was in darkness, and although the moon was

bright there was little danger of being seen unless the patrolling men returned prematurely. The second sash-window she tried opened easily and she climbed inside, closing it quietly behind her. Finding herself in a large dining-room which she could afford to ignore, she utilized the breathing space to draw the gun from a holster just above her left ankle, and set off to find Rashid's study. The villa was apparently deserted, but experience forced her to proceed with caution.

Ruti turned the door handle gingerly and pulled it open on what seemed like a hallway. She stopped for a moment to get her bearings. Almost directly in front of her was an open door through which she could see a settee, which indicated that it was probably the drawing-room. At that point her speculation was interrupted by a jolting pain in her wrist as someone knocked her gun to the floor. The shock was followed by a sharp command in Urdu.

She stopped in her tracks and straightened up. Stepping from his hiding-place 90 degrees from the other side of the door, the young man holding the gun pointed at her heart, looked as stunned as she was by their encounter. He said something to her in his own language, and when she shook her head uncomprehendingly, he switched easily to English. "Put your hands in the air," he demanded. He was excited, but in control of the situation.

Ruti obeyed, flexing her right hand and wrist in a vain effort to ease the pain, but sensing that it was only bruised. She wondered inconsequentially where Henry was.

The Pathan gestured with his gun for her to move across the hall into the drawing-room. Inside, he switched on the lights. Ruti thought for a moment it was a signal for the men in the grounds to come, but the heavy ceiling-to-floor velvet drapes were drawn, so that the light could not escape. It was remarkably pleasant. The room had been furnished in good taste and the atmosphere was ... she groped for the word ... *civilized*. It would not have come as a surprise if he had suddenly put the gun away and offered her an apéritif.

The young man was probably in his early twenties, and judging from his self-assured manner presumably no thug; she guessed he was an ideological recruit from one of the universities. He was also remarkably handsome, and she wondered if there was any significance in him being alone in the villa; whether Rashid was perhaps a homosexual.

He asked Ruti who she was, bringing her back to earth. She took her time in answering. Having been caught red-handed, breaking into the house with a gun ready for use, it was too late to bluff. She wished she had not been so cautious, and left the gun in its holster so that there was still something to fall back on. Studying her captor she sensed that he was not as relaxed as he pretended, but that he was capable nevertheless of holding on to her until others arrived. She toyed with the idea of trying to seduce him, but doubted whether it was a practical suggestion. Assuming he was not gay and took the proposition seriously, he would have to be an idiot not to tie her arms or legs first. A more practical alternative was to upset him, to destroy that veneer of composure.

"How did you know I was in the house?" she enquired mildly, as though they were comparing notes.

"The alarm system," he replied. "We used the unsealed windows like bait. If anyone opens them it triggers off a flashing red light above the television."

"I suppose that is the logical place – where anyone would be. There's no point in connecting it with any other part of the property ... "

The young man laughed, not taken in by the tack. "I must admit I was shaken when the fish turned out to be a woman. Who are you?"

"My name is Ruth."

"Mine is Shabbir. What a pity we could not have met in more agreeable circumstances ... "

"Why do you say that?"

He shrugged, embarrassed by the boldness of her stare.

Her smile was cynical. "You have ideas above your station. What makes you think I would go with a coloured man?" She had to grit her teeth to form the words, especially as his skin was no darker than that of many Israelis.

He flushed, but controlled his temper with an effort. "White women are such whores they can only think of one thing. *I* was thinking of what will happen to you when my leader gets back. Your only chance of staying alive is to tell me the truth: what are you doing here?"

"I've nothing to hide. I am with the police. A proper raid was planned originally, but no-one takes Rashid very seriously, and when we discovered the place was only guarded by a few students, we decided to cut down on numbers – and that left just me! I expect I shall get into trouble for being *too* complacent."

"You will have trouble all right!"

She pointedly ignored him. "What do *you* know about trouble? All you young idealists are good for is theory; reality is a lot tougher. When did you last kill someone? Are you capable of pulling that trigger now?"

"You can easily find out, woman."

"I meant in cold blood. I'm not stupid enough to try and jump you with these odds."

He sneered. "What odds would you consider?"

"To be really fair I should tie an arm behind my back. I am a trained officer; you are only an overgrown schoolboy feeling tough because he has a gun in his hand."

He tried to smile, but Ruti could sense that he was

fighting a losing battle with his temper. She was disappointed when he ordered her to turn round and put her hands on the wall; she wondered what he was getting at.

In fact, Shabbir was searching to see if she had another gun, although as his hands felt between her armpits and between her legs he allowed them to fumble there longer than was necessary, patently trying to humiliate her. Dismissing the empty ankle holster he ordered her to face him again. "Just a precaution," he said, "before I even up the odds." He threw his gun and hers along the floor into the hallway. Then he held up his hands. "Let us see how you can cope with an overgrown schoolboy. If I win, all I expect is an apology; if you win no doubt as a white woman you will want to take advantage of my young black body, but I'm prepared to risk that ... "

"You really are a conceited young man," Ruti remarked in a friendlier manner. But even as he was responding to her smile she suddenly attacked. In one movement she vaulted over a settee between them, her elbows and knees crunching into his body with such force that he overbalanced and slipped to the ground. She landed on top to pin him down but before she could steady herself he drew up one of his legs between them, pushed up with it and sent her flying over his head.

Cat-like, they scrambled to their feet and faced each other again. Ruti had realized from the start, and it was slowly dawning on the man, that they were evenly matched. He was considerably bigger, stronger and through some form of military training was obviously fit; Ruti, although strong by the standards of ordinary men was no match for him physically but she possessed the superior combat skills and techniques.

Initially, in his complacency the man had intended to use only the minimum of force; now he realized he was fighting for his life. They circled each other warily; neither prepared to risk an ill-timed attack.

Looking for a makeshift weapon, Ruti's outstretched hand found a wicker chair and hurled it at his head, timing her leap to compensate for his instinctive evasive action. The chair was merely intended as a distraction, and because he fell for the feint she was able to catch him on the wrong foot. Her forehead crunched into the bridge of his nose, and as his eyes filled with tears, he failed to see the follow-up stiff fingered jabs, three in quick succession. All landed on their target, one on his right eye momentarily blinding him.

The hapless Shabbir reeled back, and Ruti measured him for a kick to the groin, but he could still see with one eye and as her foot snaked out, the young man stepped inside and brought his own knee up sharply. The reaction had been instinctive; he forgot that she was not quite as vulnerable there as a man, but fortunately for him the bony part of his knee came into contact with the front of her pelvis, and the pain filtered through her groin in powerful waves. However, the intensity of her training had made her familiar with pain, and she did not allow herself to dwell on the discomfort. Conscious of a muscular arm sweeping round like a scythe, she forced life back into her rebellious legs, bringing her metal-capped heel down sharply against his instep, temporarily paralysing the foot.

Dulled with pain, both were now fighting no less determinedly, by instinct. The punishment soaked up by Shabbir might have incapacitated a lesser man, but pride enabled him to fight on, slower and more cautiously, but still dangerous. Tired almost as much from her own exertions as from his blows, Ruti began to doubt that she should last much longer.

Relying to a large extent on her greater will, she forced herself to attack again, doubling her man over by pushing the settee into his knees and jumping on to his shoulders as he stooped. But although she managed to get a stranglehold, she underestimated his strength. Despite the extra weight, Shabbir still managed to stand up, and spinning round several times, hurled himself backwards against a wall. The impact dashed every ounce of breath from Ruti's body, the room shook with the impact, and as Shabbir moved forward, dazed himself, Ruti went limp and slid to the floor.

Barely conscious, she struggled to keep her eyes focused on the man as he lurched towards her. Even so she could not avoid the kick aimed at her ribs, although the sharpness of this fresh pain shook off the overwhelming desire for unconsciousness. As Shabbir loomed overhead, Ruti wondered how she could avoid the next kick when her eyes were distracted by a flashing red light on a metal box attached to the television set.

The Pathan had his back to the box, but he was alert enough to notice the way her eyes had left him and quickly returned – too quickly. He glanced round, recognized the danger signal and headed for the hallway where he had so carelessly tossed his gun. Ruti tackled him low from behind and he lost his balance. With the benefit of surprise Ruti was able to get on top, but she no longer had the strength to restrain him and he wriggled free, raising a fist to strike at her jaw.

"Hold it there!"

Shabbir stopped, frozen by the command. Curiosity got the better of him and he looked over his shoulder at two Europeans advancing towards him. The very tall younger man had a hand menacingly in his jacket pocket as though he had just stepped from an American gangster film. He wondered why, with no reason to conceal the gun, the newcomer was prepared to shoot through the cloth of his jacket, but discretion was the better part of valour, and he remained motionless.

"Are you all right?" Henry demanded anxiously of the girl. Ruti felt like bursting into tears – rushing to put her arms round him, she contented herself with a business-like nod, but wincing as she got to her feet.

"In the nick of time," she said, trying to sound on top of the situation. "Best tradition of the U.S. Cavalry."

Crawford, who had been silent suddenly interrupted, attempting to impose his authority. "Who is this woman, Franklin? I thought the place was supposed to be empty ... ?"

Before Henry could reply, Ruti walked past him, gently massaging her ribs. "While you are performing the introductions," she told him, "I'll just get my gun from the hall."

"Oh no!" the colonel commanded. "You stay where we can keep an eye on you." He produced a gun from his pocket, and Henry guessed that the bulge at the end of the barrel was a silencer.

"Put that away!" Henry commanded, stunned by its appearance. "She's working with me."

Crawford lowered the gun only slightly, keeping it in his hand. "Who is she?"

"A 'contact' of mine – that's all you need to know."

"While you two are arguing, *please* can I get my gun?" Ruti asked wearily. "I feel naked without it."

"Yes."

"No!"

The conflicting commands were simultaneous, and the girl stopped in confusion. Henry, equally puzzled by Crawford's assertiveness protested: "Don't interfere, Colonel – this is my operation. You're here at my invitation."

"That's true, but as the senior officer present I cannot completely abdicate my authority. Either you put me completely in the picture, or I shall have to take over."

Henry suspected that his bluff was being called, but for the moment he was unable to do anything about it. "Well, if you are looking for responsibility, what are we going to do about this chap?" He gestured towards the young Pathan who remained silent on his knees, waiting for what he sensed would be his summary execution.

"Shoot him," Crawford ordered.

Shabbir's eyes closed in resignation at the command which merely confirmed his worst fears.

Henry glanced down at him helplessly. "The object of the exercise was to get in and out of here as quickly as possible, and without raising the alarm – not to start killing Rashid's men. In any case, I don't shoot people in cold blood," he told Crawford.

Crawford smiled. "I'm not as concerned with *why*, or in what circumstances you would, but *how*! You see, Franklin, I don't believe you've got a gun in that pocket."

"Don't be ridiculous."

"It occurred to me before at the flat. It had to be incredibly small to be practically hidden by your face. Not the sort of gun a man would use, especially a professional."

"This is a ridiculous conversation to be having in front of other people. I'll happily settle your curiosity later. First, we need to get this chap tied up, and start our search."

Crawford raised his gun again. "Indulge me, Franklin. I simply must know if there is anything in that pocket, apart from your fingers … "

"When Beckton hears about this … "

" … Stuff Beckton: this is *my* territory. Come on now, Franklin – call my bluff. Let's see that gun … ?"

"I don't know what you are trying to prove … ?"

Crawford shrugged imperceptibly. "One thing at a time." He turned to the kneeling man. "You! Get up and see if he has a gun ... "

The young man shook his head.

"You don't have an option. *I'll* shoot you if you don't."

Hesitantly Shabbir stood up. He did not trust the older man yet he suspected he was the more ruthless of the two Englishmen.

As he advanced on Henry, Ruti took advantage of the preoccupation to drop him with a karate chop behind his right ear. As he slumped to the ground, she turned her attention to Crawford, but the barrel of his gun was already pointing at her. She knew from his expression that he was going to squeeze the trigger, and she felt rooted to the floor, helpless in the face of death. But suddenly Henry was between them. Almost at once there was an ominous 'plop' and she knew he had stopped the bullet intended for her.

Torn between running into the hall to get her own gun, and going to Henry's assistance, Ruti hesitated. Meanwhile, Henry was struggling to resist the waves of faintness that threatened to carry him off. Distantly, through a gathering black fog he could see Crawford smiling superciliously, and uplifted by an intense anger, he summoned his reserves of energy to wrest the gun from the older man's hand. His fingers closed desperately on the colonel's wrist, but he was unable to parry the counter-punch carefully aimed at the blood-soaked patch high up on his chest. The climax of pain was enough to unbalance him in his weakened state, and he fell backwards on to the carpet.

Part of his subconscious cried out for the oblivion of unconsciousness, but he was too concerned for Ruti to let go. She was bending over him frantically, tearing his blood-stained shirt away from the bullet wound. His heart sank at their plight, knowing that he was responsible for her not retrieving her gun; the uncharacteristic indecisiveness that would cost them their lives. Nor would he even have the dying satisfaction of watching Crawford share his fate.

Ruti was busy trying to staunch the bleeding, but he looked up dispassionately as Crawford raised his gun and prepared to despatch them both. Resigned to death, Henry wondered in a completely detached way if he should not experience fear of some sort; yet his only emotion was one of frustration, and still worse the sense of failure that even his attempt to save the girl he was prepared to die for had been a failure.

Eleven

The bullet for which Henry had resigned himself failed to arrive. Instead he saw Colonel Crawford glance towards the door, and following his gaze his own eyes made out Rashid and a new bodyguard, a man as big, if not as ugly, as the late Hassan. Preoccupied as he was, Henry liked to think the replacement had some bearing on the way he had manhandled the other bodyguard at Rashid's office; Hamilton would have been proud of him.

But it was not a moment for complacency; the newcomers were scarcely a reassuring sight, and if he was going to die, he hoped it would be quick and relatively painless. The wound, high up on his chest, was painful enough, although he suspected that much of it was due to the pressure Ruti was applying in an effort to staunch the bleeding. He wanted to tell her to stop – to protest that she seemed to be making matters worse, pressing a spent bullet even further into damaged tissue – but he did not seem to have the energy to waste on speech.

He tried to catch what Rashid and Crawford were discussing so animatedly, but it was difficult to concentrate with Ruti so close, whispering words of encouragement, telling him it was only a flesh wound. He wondered if she was merely trying to reassure him, but commonsense told him she was probably right. From his proximity to the gun when it was fired the bullet must have passed straight through him. Being much taller than the other man, the trajectory of a bullet fired upwards would have taken it through his back near the collarbone. Henry's vivid imagination immediately projected some horrific pictures, until a sharp pain in his back, as though he was lying on a nail, put matters in perspective and he realized that it was probably a neat little hole, unlikely to be fatal unless he was allowed to bleed to death. He consoled himself with the thought that the most terrible wounds were relatively painless ... although he had also read somewhere that wounded men had been known to experience pain in limbs that had already been amputated.

The debate in his head was confusing and the dizziness returned, so that he had to draw on untapped reserves to stay conscious as Rashid walked over to examine him. He would not give him the satisfaction ...

Rashid's manner was mild, like a reproving schoolmaster. Nodding politely at Ruti, he squatted on his haunches next to the recumbent Henry, and smiled without humour. "My word, you do look a bit of a mess, Mr Franklin!" He paused, as though waiting for a response, before continuing: "I can't say I am sorry to see you suffering – you have been a nuisance at every turn. In fact, the sight of you is something of a consolation to me, after all the aggravation I have had today ... "

The revelation was oddly comforting to Henry. He did not have the energy to waste on banter, but he smiled.

Rashid stood up, turning to Crawford. "I wish you had shot him somewhere more unpleasant – in the stomach, or the kneecaps perhaps ... he is not suffering enough for my taste!"

Crawford sniffed disdainfully. "I'm a professional."

"Professional traitor!" Ruti corrected. She was holding Henry's hand, but with the other she gestured towards the young Pathan who was beginning to regain consciousness, and turned to Rashid. "Don't think *you* can trust him either – he tried to persuade Henry to shoot your man. *Ask* him!"

Rashid smiled mechanically. "When I need advice from Mossad, I shall ask – I'm not proud. Meanwhile, the word is inappropriate; we accept help from *anyone* if it suits us."

Henry, wondering about the significance of the last remark, began to suspect that the Pathan shared his dislike of Crawford. With an effort he addressed Rashid: "Anyone?"

Rashid looked surprised. "Oh, you've found your tongue, Mr Franklin! I thought you were sulking … "

Henry smiled. "We can't all be gracious in defeat, Mr Rashid!"

The editor inclined his head. "I must admit your behaviour has placed a great strain on my usual graciousness. Do you realize I have just flown in from Islamabad? It has been an exhausting day."

Henry sensed that he should keep Rashid talking, but he felt incredibly weak and wanted to conserve what little strength he still had. Gambling that Ruti might guess what was on his mind, he squeezed her hand, pointedly looking straight ahead, and it seemed to work.

"I don't see how you can blame that on us," she suddenly remarked, "especially since everything has ended so satisfactorily from your point of view. We are the losers."

"On the contrary. You may be the losers in the sense that you are about to die, but Mr Franklin has caused me a great deal of bother on two counts … "

"*Two* … ?" Henry echoed.

"My meeting in Islamabad today was with a very charming lady who can be most useful to the Cause. We were to talk this evening about specific ideas she might contribute, but we were interrupted by a call from my people at the *Cage D'Or*. Some idiot decided not to disturb me last night when they discovered Miss Kenan had gone, and when they rang me this morning I was already *en route* for Islamabad. With hindsight – knowing that the good colonel was deputizing for me so ably – I should have stayed to complete the discussions. The lady was most disappointed ... "

"Surely they can be resumed in the next day or so?" Crawford enquired.

"The lady will be in Europe for months."

"Oh ... well then you should have telephoned me and asked me to look into it ... "

"As a matter of fact I tried. You were not in this afternoon?"

"As it happens ... "

" ... Mr Franklin wanted to know about the second upset," Rashid interrupted, "so let me continue: not only was I expected to sort out what the idiots at the club had bungled, but I will be considerably out of pocket. As you know, the club's income benefits considerably from the earnings of our charming 'hostesses'. Thanks to Franklin we have lost the services of our best earner ... "

Dreading what he was about to hear, Henry opened his mouth to protest, but anticipating him, Rashid continued: " ... Yes ... the deceptively sweet young thing you knew as Helga! I ask you, gentlemen: she disappears at the busiest time of the evening and turns up later with some fantastic story about being kidnapped! It was quite well planned. Her shoes and stockings were scratched and splashed with mud – which might have fooled my men on the spot if it was not for the money sticking out of her bra – the bribe you gave her ... "

"You cynical bastard!" Ruti cried. "It was no bribe – it was her savings. Henry found that money and used it to coerce her into helping us."

Rashid shrugged. "Too bad. But if we *were* wrong, she was

just as guilty on another score – of robbing us in the first place. The girls are paid well; there is no need to bite the hand that feeds them. We cannot help but be suspicious of people who put money before anything else.''

"What about Crawford then?" Ruti interjected. "You don't imagine he shares your *ideals*. Ask your man what he thinks ... ''

She was referring to Shabbir who was now sitting up, rubbing the back of his head. He looked up at Rashid apologetically before offering an explanation. "There were three of them. I overpowered the girl who arrived first, but the younger man – the one who has been shot – came up behind me with a gun ... ''

"He didn't have a gun – you damned fool!" Crawford said, his manner quiet but contemptuous.

Ignoring him, Shabbir continued to report to his leader. "I *thought* he had a gun – it was in his pocket."

Rashid sighed. "What happened?"

"There was a bulge in his jacket pocket and he behaved as though it was a gun. It would have never have occurred to me to question it, until this man did. They were together so what he said confused me – especially since he had already told him to get rid of me. I thought it was a trap. Then he drew a gun and threatened to shoot me himself if I refused, so I ... When my attention was distracted, the girl must have hit me from behind ... ''

Rashid spoke to him in Urdu, and the young man relaxed and seemed to speak more freely without the fear of being contradicted by the authoritative Crawford. Eventually Rashid had heard enough, and he nodded with satisfaction.

Fearing the worst, Ruti appealed to him to let Henry go. "He needs to be in hospital. There's nothing he can do to harm you now. He was going back to England anyway."

Rashid laughed. "I was just about to enquire if you had a

last request, but that is too much to ask."

With an effort, Henry propped himself up against the wall so that he had a less distorted view of the room. In the seconds it took to regain his breath he kept his eyes on Crawford, but when he spoke the request was directed at Rashid. "I've got one that is reasonable. You don't like traitors any more than me. Give me a gun so that I can kill that bastard before I die ... "

The colonel shrugged at his vehemence. "You are a poor loser, Franklin. Even Beckton would give me credit for the way in which I've handled this whole affair. There is not a man at the High Commission, or in London, who doesn't think I'm just a pompous old idiot waiting for my pension. And while I've been encouraging that belief over the past few years, I have made enough money to keep *them* all in pensions ... "

"Money!" spat Henry.

"There was the challenge too. Proving that I could outwit them all. Who do you think provided the brains of this growing organization – Rashid here? I don't dispute he is a good man. He'll go far, but he doesn't have my experience, my *background*."

Henry, watching the Pathan's reaction, noticed the muscles in his jaw contract at the patronizing asides, and he was not surprised when Rashid chipped in: "Wait a moment, Colonel! While I cannot allow Mr Franklin's last request, I have no wish to rub salt into his wounds. Since he hates you so much it must be agonizing for him to feel that his demise is no more than a homage to your greater glory. I think it only fair to admit to him that you have overstated your own importance a little ... "

"What is that supposed to mean?" demanded Crawford.

"Just that it is depressing enough for a man to know he has lost; more so to believe that he has lost to the man he hates most in the world. His soul would never rest in peace, tortured by such a falsehood."

"What falsehood?"

"That you were sent by Allah to lead his children out of the wilderness; that you are the mastermind behind this movement. You may have hoodwinked *your* people, not mine. You have been useful to us – I cannot deny that – and for that I have suffered your less than endearing manner. It was only because I put the organization before personal vanity, that I have not made an issue of it before. It does not matter *who* the leader is – so long as he does his job properly. Even you cannot be satisfied with your recent performance."

"What on earth do you mean by that?" Crawford demanded.

"It was you who persuaded me that the British Government would do a deal on some of the stolen manuscripts – that they would pay well if they believed they were getting some valuable intelligence on the Islamic cause thrown in. But you were hoist on your own petard! Instead of leaving the negotiations to you, they sent two agents to get what they wanted for nothing ... "

"I admit that was a miscalculation," Crawford conceded, "but it was corrected almost immediately. You would never have got rid of a top man like Hamilton without me. And don't forget it was you who let Franklin slip through your fingers ... "

"That is the difference between us. I accept my responsibilities – and the blame when things go wrong. The arrival of Hamilton and Franklin caused us to over-react, I admit. Several people have died, and today we had to kill the lovely Helga ... Now I suppose that we must dispose of Franklin and Miss Kenan ... "

Crawford hesitated. "Of course ... you're not suggesting that we allow them to go free!"

"No, it was inevitable. I do not question the necessity; merely the state of affairs which led to them. I believe one should endeavour to anticipate problems and therefore handle them with finesse. Now, with the deaths of three more foreign nationals on their hands, the police will not only be sorely embarrassed – which will make them crack down on all and sundry – but you will have some explaining to do to your people in London." When the colonel made no reply, he continued mildly enough: "You see, my dear Crawford, if D16 has any doubts at all about your loyalty – and you can be sure Franklin has seen to that – then his death, their second agent to die in your territory, could be the straw that breaks the camel's back. Remember, your value to us exists only as long as you are trusted in London, and we have one foot in the enemy camp so to speak."

Crawford stirred nervously and fingered the trigger of the gun that was still in his hand. "Are you threatening me, Rashid?"

Rashid's response was interrupted by the sound of gunfire in the grounds. He snapped a command in Urdu to his two men and they dashed to the window, peering anxiously through either side of the curtains into the darkness.

Henry would have liked to mock their discomfiture, but in his weakened state it seemed too much of an effort. At least he had the satisfaction of knowing that Khan and his men were around. If the inspector had decided to adopt a more positive stance he undoubtedly had the manpower to storm the villa if necessary – although whether they would be in time to save him and Ruti was another matter.

It was the constant activity that prevented Henry from losing consciousness, and there was yet another surprise in store. Suddenly filling the open doorway was a stranger with an automatic in his hand. A European in a well-tailored tan suit, he looked relaxed, even happy, and his first words left no doubt as to his nationality. " 'Evening all!' "

Only slightly more aggressively he told the Pakistanis by the window to put their hands in the air, but from the glint in his eyes it was very apparent he was not the sort of man to argue with. He took in the room at a glance, noting the recumbent Henry, but saying nothing, and regarding everyone with the same benign interest. "Who was threatening whom?" he enquired politely. "Please carry on: don't let me spoil the party."

Crawford's relief was evident. "You're English, thank God! You must be Hamilton's replacement. I'm Colonel Crawford from the High Commission ... "

"I thought you were, old boy. In fact I think I can recognize everyone except for the two goons, and that delightful young lady holding Franklin's hand. I should be so lucky ... "

"Don't be fooled by her looks – she's damned dangerous; a Mossad agent," Crawford protested. "Look, I'll explain everything later; we've got to get this man to the hospital before he bleeds to death ... "

The newcomer approached Henry, as though he was only just aware of his condition. "I've heard about *you* ... seems you're on Beckton's conscience. He'll blame me for this ... who shot you ... ?"

"*They* did, of course," Crawford interjected. He had no time to complete the sentence. As though by a pre-arranged signal Rashid fired from his jacket pocket – hitting the Englishman in the chest. Fitted with a silencer, the report made no appreciable noise and Henry was entranced by the unreal effect as Crawford sank in slow motion to his knees, and then fell forward on to his face.

The shot had been so unexpected – and ironic after the scene Crawford had made, inferring that professionals were not afraid to show their guns – that for a split second everyone seemed frozen in suspended animation. By the time Beckton's man reacted he had lost the initiative. As his finger tightened on the trigger, Rashid's giant bodyguard had leapt in front of his master. The roar of the unsilenced gun made the windows rattle, and in contrast to Crawford's demise, it seemed perfectly natural for the Pakistani to be thrown in the air and dashed like a doll to the ground.

Two deaths, almost instantaneously, seemed to freeze the occupants of the room into a nightmarish tableau as Henry struggled to keep his eyes open, before Ruti shattered it by suddenly leaving him and running into the hallway to find her gun. A moment later the younger bodyguard was grappling with Beckton's man, preventing him from drawing a bead on Rashid. Rashid was unable to fire without risking the life of his own man.

Only as Ruti returned like the avenging angel she had seemed to Henry when they first met, did Rashid act decisively. Knowing that she was probably the better shot, he pointed his gun at Henry. "Drop it!" he commanded her, "or I shall finish him off."

The girl hesitated, desperately hoping that Beckton's man would decide the issue for her by overpowering his opponent but he seemed to be making heavy weather of it. At the second command from Rashid she dropped her gun.

"Come here!" he ordered.

By the time she had reached him Beckton's man had incapacitated the less experienced Pathan, but too late to prevent Rashid from holding the gun to her head, and ordering them to keep their distance. Henry watched in terror as Hamilton's replacement slowly raised his automatic and took careful aim at the retreating Rashid who was holding Ruti in front of him like a shield.

"Don't shoot – for God's sake!" he begged. The command was desperate but the words came through as little more than a croak; luckily the room was momentarily quiet and the agent heard him. He looked across at Henry, concerned. "He'll get away ... ?"

"The police will pick him up," said Henry. "They are in the grounds."

The agent fumed with frustration as Rashid continued to back out of the room, still protected by the girl. Warning the Englishman not to follow him, he disappeared into the hallway, and then realizing that Ruti would only be an encumbrance to him, threw her off and headed for the front door. As soon as she returned, the agent took off in pursuit, ordering her to telephone for an ambulance – but she had already anticipated him.

In hospital, Franklin had his best night's sleep in weeks; not waking until two o'clock the next afternoon, by which time there was a queue of people waiting to see him. To the man from the High Commission he pleaded loss of memory, claiming to have no idea how or why he had come to be shot. He did not expect to be believed, but nor would the truth have seemed any more likely, so he did not have anything to lose. However, his act – no doubt aided by the reality of a hospital bed – was convincing enough and the diplomat was sympathetic.

At least it worked until Henry forgot his role for a moment when the Foreign Office man offered to arrange for visitors to be kept away so that he could rest. Henry agreed weakly. "I don't think I'm up to facing strangers yet. The only people I want to see when they arrive are Miss Kenan and Inspector Khan."

The diplomat's surprise at hearing names turned to one of disdain. "Oh, I suppose you're one of them ... "

"*Them?*"

"Cloak and dagger."

"As a matter of fact, I'm a librarian."

"Of course."

Inspector Khan was in a good mood considering that Rashid seemed to have escaped. "There is a nationwide alert, but he's gone to ground – probably had an escape route prepared for such an emergency. I wouldn't be surprised if he was in Egypt by now. At least he will be out of our hair … "

"What a pity that he left Islamabad prematurely. I don't suppose Miss Byoussi had much time to loosen his tongue?"

Khan shrugged. "We have something on tape; nothing dramatically subversive or incriminating, but enough – at least, for the authorities to realize where his true sentiments lie. The paper will be closed for a start … and when *we* catch up with him there will be a number of criminal charges arising from last night."

"If you are happy, then I am too. I don't feel any special animosity towards Rashid. He's an unscrupulous bastard, but at least he's sincere."

Khan laughed. "It's that sort of naïvety which at times makes me wonder if you're not a librarian after all. Some of the most vicious crimes have been conducted by people who are sincere – you have only to look at our Muslim brothers in Iran … "

The inspector was turning to leave when he appeared to remember something significant. "I nearly forgot … If you can put Rashid the idealist out of your head for a moment and try to think in terms of Rashid the common criminal, didn't you once tell me about a conversation with him about stolen Arabic manuscripts?"

"That's right. He has taken to collecting them – but not for the usual reasons of antiquity. He has a contempt for Western values; what he regards as our obsession with the aesthetic, the works of art, the baubles … "

"So what is his interest?"

"Oh, he is not above *using* such 'baubles' – for raising money. His main interest is in the historic symbolism that some of them offer to the Islamic cause."

"Well, perhaps you can help us again with a more pleasant problem. In our search of the villa we found a cache of manuscripts, and some very early printed books. There seems no doubt they must have been stolen."

"Some of them are from Britain. Now I can admit I came to find and identify them."

"If you can be specific I can arrange for the curator at the National Museum to go through them with you in a day or so."

When Ruti was shown in, his euphoria was replaced by anxiety. The decks were now clear: would she now be free to come back to England with him? Or had it all been just a dream? The initial reaction to her presence in the room resolved his personal fears. He knew he still wanted her. Did she still want him?

"I love you," she conceded. "I would like nothing better than to spend the rest of our lives together ... "

"But?"

Ruti shrugged. "I don't know. It's all happened so suddenly. The major decisions in life are never simply black or white." She told him of the discussion with Deutsch. "He wants me to go home – take a vacation for a few months – to collect my thoughts ... "

"Is that what you want to do?" he asked, gently.

"No." She shook her head, as though to demonstrate her conviction. "I want to be with you."

"Then what is the problem? Together, we would be happy."

She bent over to kiss his lips, and smiled at his surprised expression.

"What was that for?" he enquired.

"Does there have to be a reason? I love you ... "

"And you're scared it's a daydream?"

"I'm just scared – period. Just tell me what I should do, Henry, and I'll do it. I trust you."

"You mean, if I order you to come to England, you will? I thought Israeli women were emancipated? I don't understand. What prevents you from making your own decision?"

"Because of the possibility that there might be an element of truth in what my boss said about personal responsibility. Is my need as great as my country's?"

"I can understand your apprehension ... loyalty is a virtue ... "

"No, you cannot understand," she interjected. "The Intelligence business is a game to the great powers; deadly but still a game. But when a nation's existence is threatened it is fighting for its life. Every person who drops out leaves a gap in its defences."

"But that could go on for ever. You'd be sacrificing your future for a cause – not survival. Israel is too powerful to be threatened any more. But some of your leaders think in terms of a greater Israel. That is a Cause. Why is that so different to what Rashid believes?"

"The difference between right and wrong."

"Come off it, Ruti. Khan just accused me of being naïve. But I'm not as bad as you. Intelligence is a dirty business, and gradually you'll become contaminated. Even if you believed in the premise of good guys and bad guys, and you don't mind shooting the Crawfords and Rashids, what happens when you're told to knock off the good guys too?"

Ruti wriggled, embarrassed, under his stare. "We are not like that," she protested.

He smiled cynically. "Wait and see, darling. Apart from the fact that for most of the time it is difficult to differentiate between allies and enemies, the ends have a habit of justifying the means, and before you know where you are the values have changed. After the Lebanon War in '82, the Christian Phalangists were the only remaining cohesive force of any significant size, and they had always been allies of the Israelis, yet I've even heard it speculated that the assassination of their leader Gemayal, the new President-elect, was arranged by Mossad ... "

"That is the sort of rumour spread by our enemies."

"But it makes sense. The Israelis knew that he was too unbending to survive for long, and his death was a convenient excuse for them to go back in and complete their mop-up operations. It's what I said about the ends justifying the means."

She smiled. "Darling, we are having our first quarrel."

He squeezed her hand. "I want you to do what is right for you in the long term; but you mustn't settle for a future over which you will never have any control."

She shrugged. "I'm not even sure I have anything to offer any more – at least, at what we call the 'sharp end'. I went to pieces last night. On two separate occasions I hesitated, and lost the initiative – something that had never happened to me before."

"All I remember is that you put my life before the job – is that so terrible?"

"Of course not. But I can't have it both ways. My priorities have to be clear cut ... "

"And what about settling down and having children?"

"That is all part of the maze. It has been suggested by someone I respect that I step back and try to evaluate the situation more rationally. It would seem to make sense. Perhaps it would be just as valid for you to do the same. You know what they say about holiday romances?"

"Holiday?" He groaned. "It seems I've been here for ever."

Postscript

Incredibly, the only unreal experience in a three-week spell of fantasy was coming home – to the prospect of behaving naturally with friends and colleagues whose perception of the daily routine of life was unaltered. Nice people, but incapable of comprehending any world outside their own, any more than he had once been – although he had, at least, always given rein to a vivid imagination. The post-coital discussion with Ruti on the subject of the real world seemed only yesterday. Now he knew only one thing for certain – that Ruti apart – he was glad to be back.

Having forbidden all mention of Pakistan, Beckton had provided him with a cover story: a UNESCO sponsored conference in Paris on child literacy. The conference was genuine enough; Henry was supplied with a comprehensive written report and instructed to read it in detail, so that he could answer questions if called upon. It was an eerie experience to see his name listed among the delegates, and he wondered if D16 had bothered to send someone to impersonate him.

The ordeal he feared most was facing Heather – or to be more precise it was fear of the initial telephone call announcing his return. He had reason to be apprehensive. Leaving aside a guilty conscience over his feelings for Ruti, his failure to keep in touch must have seemed inexcusable to someone not in possession of the facts. Heather had a telephone by her bed, and even if he had been occupied every hour of the working day, he could have contacted her at night. Furthermore, she might well have thought Paris was so near he could have flown back at a weekend – or even asked her to join him for a couple of days.

Recognizing that she had every reason to feel snubbed, Henry's immediate problem was how to respond to the inevitable recriminations. He knew he was sufficiently on the defensive to over-react to criticism, yet he was not prepared to endure it in silence – especially as he was too honest not to want to resolve the dilemma as soon as possible. It was certainly impossible to remain silent for six months, waiting for Ruti's decision.

He spent near enough fifteen minutes rehearsing what he would say, but when he actually heard Heather's voice on the line, panic parched his mouth and throat so that he could speak only with difficulty. Scrapping the prepared speech, he settled for an uncomfortable " ... It's me ... " When she did not respond immediately, he probed tentatively for a response: "Heather ... ?"

She sighed, it seemed with relief. "Henry!"

" ... How are you?"

"I'm fine. How are you?" She broke off with a nervous laugh. "Listen to us – stuck for words! There's so much I wanted to say ... I've missed you."

He was on the point of echoing her last remark, but the words stuck in his throat. "I had no idea it would take so long ... I ... "

"You're back – that's all that matters. Are you too tired to pop over – or shall I come to you?"

The ice broken, the physical reunion was much easier. Heather demonstrated her joy at his return in the most affectionate manner leaving little time for questions and explanations. Henry was overwhelmed despite the minor hitch which arose when he took off his shirt to reveal the two small dressings over his fast-healing wound. He got by with a garbled excuse about being caught in swing doors and being cut very slightly by broken glass; Heather seemed too preoccupied to expect a fuller explanation. In fact when they made love, her ardour was surprising and more than a little emotional.

Heather possessed the sort of beauty that demanded reverence – or at the very least respectful handling – which had an inhibiting effect on all but the most insensitive lovers. Their relationship had been quite normal, but it seemed that she could never lose that last vestige of reserve. The difference was startling and he could not help remarking on it.

For some time Heather refused to answer and, contented, he was prepared to let the issue slide. He was beginning to doze off before she spoke at last. Lying on her back, she might have been addressing the ceiling. "I missed you ... "

Henry squeezed her hand. "If I could look forward to this sort of homecoming every time, I'd willingly go away more often."

"You could – as long as I knew you were coming back."

He raised himself on one elbow. "What does that mean?"

She stared up at him. "I thought you had left for good. You disappeared without a word ... "

"Someone was supposed to phone you."

"It's hardly the same. I got it into my head that you couldn't face me; that there had been an opportunity to escape, and you jumped at it."

"Why should I want to run away?"

She smiled. "It seems silly now, but for some time I've been conscious of being too demanding, of being a nagger."

"You're ambitious for me. That's not a terrible thing if it's kept in perspective."

"But that's it, precisely."

"And you imagined the worm had turned?"

She kissed his cheek. "I would never have fallen in love with a worm."

"What did you fall in love with?"

"*What* ... as opposed to whom?" She thought for a moment, obviously rejecting the initial images. "I would say something warm and furry ... cuddly ... a teddy bear."

"Teddy bear!" he exclaimed with disappointment. "What's wrong with a knight of the Round Table? Sir Galahad or Sit Lancelot du Lac?"

She wrinkled her nose. "They might have looked all right, but beauty is only skin deep, and it must have been bloody uncomfortable being in the same bed with all that cold, not to say *rusty* armour ... "

"I was thinking more in symbolic terms."

She giggled. "Why do men always need to be reassured about their masculinity? Well, if my teddy bear isn't virile enough for your sense of pride I'd say that tonight you were more like a *tiger*."

He found the image more acceptable. Recalling the very different life he had led for the past fortnight or so, he wondered if it showed. "Is there really no change in me?" he enquired.

She sat up and studied him carefully. " ... Change? You've caught the sun a little, perhaps, but you look exactly the same. I wouldn't want you any different."

The stolen manuscripts had been returned, discreetly and with the minimum of publicity, although it was not long before Henry heard about it on the grapevine. He had been ordered by Beckton to keep a low profile for the duration, which was no problem in view of the backlog of work at the County Library, but he was not allowed to forget the manuscripts.

During a commonplace phone call to his friend Doug Johnson, in York, Henry congratulated him on the return of Ahhidi's "Diwan". The reference led to the startling news that local police had just arrested a small-time burglar who had confessed to a number of additional crimes – including the theft of the "Diwan" and other manuscripts at the College of Oriental Studies.

Having imagined that the thefts were carried out by Arab or Asian students working to a brief, Henry was stunned. Trying to contain his excitement he pressed Johnson for further details, but he was to be disappointed.

"What details?" his friend demanded. "As far as the police are concerned ours was just one of a dozen burglaries, and since he volunteered his guilt they are not interested in the 'why's and wherefores'."

"I can see that it's just another statistic to them, but it was a bit more than that to you. Didn't you *want* to know more?"

"The only thing that concerned me was that our manuscripts had turned up, undamaged."

"But it's not as simple as that. For a start, there's no connection between their recovery and the arrest of the burglar ... "

"What gave you that idea?"

Henry floundered, realizing that he was making assumptions based on information he was not supposed to have. "That seems to be the general impression," he asserted. "Didn't you just say that this rush of conscience happened a couple of weeks *after* you had your goodies back?"

"That's true, I suppose. But it's all water under the bridge. The police told me how he got in, so we've taken appropriate steps."

" … Locked the stable door? Sounds a bit like going through the motions."

"Thank you for that vote of confidence," Johnson responded curtly.

"Come off it, Doug! It's what someone else might say – behind your back. For heaven's sake, people like us have a commitment to stop thieves – if *we* don't, then nobody else will."

"I *should* have asked for chapter and verse," Johnson admitted. "I was so relieved, I didn't think very coherently."

"It's not too late. Look, could you do me a favour? I'm thinking of presenting a paper on security at the next conference, and if you have no objection I might use the manuscripts as a case history. The police obviously won't talk to me, but you are an interested party so they would have to answer your questions. And since their petty thief is pleading guilty, they shouldn't object to you talking to him as well if he's in custody locally."

"What is *he* going to tell me?"

"*Why* he did it? Why would a small-time thief go for rare manuscripts? Where did he think he was going to sell them? It would be interesting to see if someone put him up to it … "

Henry's hunch proved correct. Johnson rang him back a week later to concede that the theories had been substantiated. "He said he might be able to identify the man if he saw him again, but he couldn't be sure. He assumed the man was a collector because he was paid one hundred and fifty pounds for what was for him a doddle. Quite a brainwave of yours, Henry. Any ideas who the mystery man is? I told the police but they didn't seem very interested."

In professing his ignorance, Henry was lying. Convinced now that Beckton was behind the thefts, he had no illusions that it could ever be proved. He recalled that Rashid had never admitted being responsible, although he was not above theft on his own doorstep. In retrospect it seemed likely that the scheme had been Crawford's. Knowing that there was an interest in very old manuscripts, he had probably persuaded London that they could be used to 'buy' vital intelligence, as well as providing him with an opportunity to infiltrate the Movement. Playing both ends against the middle, Crawford had probably made a profit on the deal, and then fed London with information they needed – some genuine but mostly fabricated – about Rashid and some of his rival groups.

He had come unstuck by underestimating Beckton's ruthlessness – sending Hamilton to get the manuscripts once their purpose had been achieved. Henry suspected that his own involvement initially had been genuine; that they needed someone to make sure that the right material was brought back. Beckton's probable guilt was a fact of life, and there was nothing he could do about it, but he objected to having been used as a pawn. The least he could do was to confront Beckton and prove that he was not as simple as they imagined.

Henry rang the only number he had, but got the high-pitch tone that indicated it was unobtainable. Checking with the operator he was told that it was a 'ceased' line; she was unable to tell him the name of the original subscriber. He rang the Foreign Office main switchboard but it seemed there was no record of any 'Mr Beckton' on their lists. It was at that moment that he realized with a sense of helplessness that Beckton's link with D16 was an assumption he had made without any evidence to support it. He could belong to any number of Intelligence departments – if indeed he worked for the government at all!

Henry decided to cut his losses and push the entire episode from his mind. Inevitably, the situation was confused. His feelings for Ruti were real enough, yet after three months' absence she occupied his thoughts less frequently. In fact, he was beginning to daydream about Heather. It was possible he was falling in love with her again – for the first time, perhaps.

The issue was resolved by fate. It had been a fairly routine day in the library until Betty Mailer, the teenager who had stopped growing at 4 feet 9 inches, complained she was unable to get a book from the stockroom; it was on the top shelf and none of the large mobile ladders was available. Henry was really too busy to deal with minor problems of this nature but he disliked keeping customers waiting, and knowing there was an ordinary stepladder available he volunteered to get the book himself.

Despite his height he discovered to his embarrassment that even he could not reach the book without balancing precariously on the hand rail above the top rung. He climbed the steps somewhat gingerly, suddenly aware of the irony of a situation in which an ordinary ladder could present difficulties while in Karachi he had shinned up a drainpipe and jumped from that onto a window sill several feet away. The memory of his prowess when the chips were down was pleasurable, and he wished Heather and the others at the library could have seen him then. It all came back vividly. He tensed the muscles in his legs as the incident was recalled in minute detail. He had jumped sideways ... or was it out ... ?

When Henry fell off the ladder, he was lucky to escape with a broken ankle. As he waited for the ambulance, the pain was intense, but he welcomed it as a means of lessening the humiliation. It was amazing how many of his staff, too busy to help Betty ten minutes earlier, were suddenly free to witness his physical fall from grace, and how members of the public seemed to have the time to spare to watch this latest illustration of man's natural indignity. Heather's uncontrolled anxiety did little to assist his morale – until he heard a couple of male voices expressing envy at the way he was being fussed over by a woman who – they speculated – could only have been a film star. Rather to his surprise, he suddenly had no objection to being kissed in full view of their audience.

"The sooner we get married, the better," she whispered. "It scares me to think what could happen without me to look after you."

It was funny; it had never occurred to him before, but if Ruti reminded him of an avenging angel, then Heather was surely the angel of mercy. The anomaly was that the English rose wanted to protect him; the Amazon to *be* protected.

The choice would have tested the wisdom of Solomon, but suddenly he knew where his destiny lay ...